WITCHFOLK

RENAE L. MOORE

Copyright

Library of Congress Control Number: 2024926927

ISBN: 979-8-9922505-0-3 (ebook)

979-8-9922505-1-0 (Paperback)

Book Cover by Renae L. Moore

First Edition 2025

10 9 8 7 6 5 4 3 2 1

Dedication

∞

For my mom, Linda
who always believed in me
especially when I didn't believe in myself.
Thank you for everything,
especially the trips to the bookstore.

∞

Historical Note

1764 – Mass exodus from village of Detroit for new settlement, population is reduced

1769 – A British lieutenant buys Hog Island (Belle Isle) from Native Americans

1783 – Michigan becomes part of the United States on September 3rd

1787 – Slavery is banned in Michigan

1861 – The Civil War starts; Michigan sends volunteers to Washington, D.C.

1862 – Thomas Edison begins working as a telegraph operator in Michigan

1865 – The Detroit Public Library opens with 5,000 books in circulation

-Detroit Historical Society (detroithistorical.org)

History of the Michigan Kingdom by Anon. Monk (1865)

1764 – A plague devastates the population of Detroit

1769 – Circe and Medusa make a haven on Belle Isle for beings cursed by the Greek gods

1783 – King Wesley Silverby creates the Michigan Kingdom; first binding cuffs used

1787 – Queen Celeste Silverby is stoned for leading a rebellion against the tyrant king

1861 – King Troy dies in a peacekeeping mission to Chicago; Queen Dawn rules as regent

1862 – Queen Dawn bans communication with America

1865 – King Elios orders the burning of the libraries

Now

1893 – Princess Amber Silverby's Freedom Movement forms in Detroit

"Fair is foul, and foul is fair."
WILLIAM SHAKESPEARE
MACBETH, Act 1, Scene 1

1

"The kingdom shall not permit a witch to live freely." Throughout the temple courtyard, the kingdom's motto echoed in a monotone loop over the loudspeaker. A clockwork boy pushed a hover cart filled with pears through the sparse crowd. He took coins from greedy hands in exchange for his wares. The gathering in the courtyard was smaller than she expected. Hope welled in her chest that maybe the public had lost their taste for the witch executions. Perhaps there would be no basket lunches on red checkerboard blankets today. No children laughing while playing with their witch hunter dolls. No fight to get the best body parts for crafting charms and curses. She hoped against hope that preparations for the upcoming royal foxhunt weren't the only reason the crowd was thin.

Amber took a deep breath to slow her racing heart. Every month, the royal guards increased their patrols and raids in the days before the foxhunt. They used the time to round up the witches who would be prey for the hunters in the labyrinth. The stonings always happened during the closing ceremony. Something had changed.

"Why do you think they're stoning her now? Why not wait?" Jasmine shook her head.

"No rest for the wicked," Amber mumbled.

Kane elbowed her. She elbowed him back and shot him a withering glance. As usual, his face was unreadable, but she felt the warning in his nudge. He was big on keeping up royal appearances, much like her mother. But Amber was too weary, to keep pretending like this was normal. It was bad enough she was forced to watch witchfolk hunted for sport in some stupid foxhunt game. It was a whole other nightmare to watch one of her friends be turned into a living statue.

"This is a bad idea, princess. We shouldn't be here," Kane whispered. Ever the protector, his eyes darted back and forth as he scanned the crowd for threats.

"The least we can do is watch. She is part of the coven," Amber whispered back. "Unless you forgot."

"That is exactly why we shouldn't be here. What if she calls out to you for help?"

"She wouldn't. No one in the coven wo —"

"What if Gav —"

"Shh," Jasmine warned. "Not here. Not now." Her eyes darted to the stage.

Amber stole a glance at the stage. Her cousin Nazim, the spare prince, stood with a trio of witch hunters. They were laughing, eating pears, and passing a flask back and forth. Nazim's training was going as well as could be expected with those bottom feeders. Last month he quit the Guild Academy and joined the hunt with the other academy rejects and dropouts. Now he had no crown and no wand. An ordinary charmless mundane.

The loudest among them was their leader, Gavin Wade, the Butcher. He was the arrogant son of her mom's rival guildmaster. His team was responsible for more than half the witch arrests the past month. A morally bankrupt group known to torture witchfolk and chop them into parts for sale on the black-market. If they couldn't have power, they would take it away from others. They unironically called themselves the Boneheads. *Magicless and stupid.* The best combination for creating the worst people in the kingdom.

Gavin looked at her with a glint in his ice blue eyes. He blew her a kiss with a wink. She flipped him off. It'd been two months since he discovered her secret, and he still hadn't made a move. *What's he waiting for?* The urge to claw out his eyes flooded her mind. She twisted her grandmother's ring. The enchanted bloodstone pulsed against her skin in synch with her throbbing temples. Her breathing slowed as her mind cleared. Accidentally shifting into her familiar now would be a mistake. She had to stay in control. One wandering thought and all their plans would be ruined. She looked away as the other boneheads burst into laughter again.

"Fine." Amber crossed her arms. The argument could wait. Afterall, she was right. No need to rush to prove it.

A hush fell over the crowd as the royal axman walked onto the stage. Amber knew Dale Wade by reputation only. And what she knew wasn't great. He was dressed in the same black guard uniform as Kane. His blonde hair was cropped short in the front and hung past his shoulders in the back. The black and red dragon mascot of the fire guild shone bright against his pale neck. The guild sigil was identical to her own neck tattoo. The same symbol decorated the handle of his quicksilver dagger.

Once Dale stood at center stage, the guest of dishonor was ushered out by two guards. Amber focused on her breathing as she watched Rynn walk across the stage. The quicksilver cuffs on her wrists glistened in the afternoon sun. Rynn who had a smile like sunshine and a temper like a tempest; much like her own. Rynn who was caught running a mission for the Medusa coven. Rynn who Amber had sent on the mission that got her caught. Amber fought back the urge to engulf the stage in flames and choke out the guards with smoke. *That was not how a royal should act.* At least according to her mom. So, Amber did what she could and made a mental note of each of their faces. Now wasn't the time to act but they would eventually get what they deserved. She would make sure of it.

A pear flew across the stage, striking Rynn in the nose. Her khaki skin turned red from the impact. Amber's chest tightened. Her familiar beat its wings against her rib cage. She didn't have to look to know who had thrown the fruit. Nazim's group erupted in laughter as blood ran down Rynn's face. A faint orange glow radiated from his ring. Damn boneheads and their charmtek. To Rynn's credit, her head didn't move, her shoulders didn't droop. Rynn stayed stoic, unmovable, her gaze fixed on a distant point at the far end of the courtyard. The breeze blew her black curls in a whirl around her tanned face. It was the only proof she wasn't a statue. Yet. *Medusa, let the pain meant for Rynn backfire and be felt by her punishers.* She added Nazim and his hunter cronies to her mental payback list.

Dale took a step to the front of the stage. He picked up the pear, took a big bite then spit the chunk in Rynn's face. A smirk twisted his face into a mask of unchecked authority that turned her stomach. As his sapphire eyes scanned the crowd, Amber shifted her gaze to her boots. No breathing exercises could calm her while she stared into the face of evil. He cleared his throat before he spoke.

"God fortify the King."

"God fortify the King." The crowd responded in unison.

He continued, "The kingdom shall not permit a witch to live freely. This is the first command of Kingslaw. A command that protects every Michigan citizen from witches and their unholy witchcraft. Today is the royal foxhunt, the most sacred of days where witches are gifted with the chance to repent for their crimes against the crown. I can think of no better way of celebrating than by honoring the king's command. This is the witch, Rynn Jilani. It was caught by hunter Wade outside the palace during the witching hour. It is believed it was plotting to kill the king. By the power of King Elios the Tinkerer, it is ordered that this monster be blessed with Medusa's Favor."

Amber knew better than to blink or she would miss her chance. With one swift movement, he thrust the quicksilver dagger towards Rynn's chest. She made her move simultaneously. *Reddo consilio.* The words echoed in her mind as she silently cast the spell. The dagger touched Rynn's chest above her heart then recoiled as if pulled back by a string. Gasps erupted from the people standing nearest the stage. In the span of a heartbeat, the dagger flipped and plunged itself hilt deep into the axman's chest. Dale's eyes widened at the impact. More gasps. Jasmine grabbed Amber's left hand and squeezed. Another heartbeat passed. Dale's blue eyes widened as he watched silver spread from the blade to his chest like spilled water. Recognition flashed in his eyes. The cursed fate he wished for Rynn was his to bear. He fell backwards under the weight of the stone. He wouldn't be returning to the royal barracks tonight. Instead, the monster would find a new home in the stonegarden amongst the other victims of Medusa's Favor.

Amber's heart skipped a beat. *The backfire spell worked. Her backfire spell. Shit. Her mom was gonna be pissed*. A half dozen guards stormed the stage. They grabbed Rynn and rushed her off as chaos erupted in the courtyard.

"Let's go," Kane grabbed her right hand. "Now."

Amber didn't argue. Kane's duty was to protect her. There was no time for any games or arguments. Jasmine kept a tight grip on her hand as they let Kane clear a path for them. She stole a glance at Gavin as they made their way out of the courtyard. He was on his knees, mouth agape, eyes fixed on his brother, the stoneman.

Amber repressed a smile.

Thank you, Medusa.

2

Princess Selene spun the silver meditation balls through her fingers and along the back of her knuckles. She listened to Amber's report of the courtyard incident with a faraway gaze. Despite the warmth in the cottage, Amber's arms were speckled with goosebumps. Between being under her mother's gaze and sitting on the cursed grounds of Belle Isle, unease made her belly churn. The stonegarden filled with living statues surrounded them on all sides. Amber felt the stares of all the cursed souls there despite being inside.

The loose blonde curls framing Selene's alabaster face fluttered with each breath. It was the same deep breathing she taught Amber to use for focusing her power. A knot formed in her stomach as she watched her mother across the table. The fast rhythm of the twirling balls set her nerves on edge. Amber blinked hard when her mother suddenly dropped the balls into their case causing the lid to slam shut.

"I'm disappointed." With a sigh Selene turned her attention to the man seated to her left, "Captain Vaughn?"

"Official word is that Rynn used a curse to attack Wade. All hints that she survived Medusa's Favor have been silenced," Tarkan said. "Regardless, she is being kept in isolation at the old jail. The guards are spooked. They won't go near her. I put Bowen on her detail, if anything happens, we'll know. She's unharmed, for now."

"Good." Selene tapped a long red nail against the table. "Make sure it stays that way. As long as they think she's to blame for the attack on the axman they won't look," Selene's eyes flicked to Amber, "elsewhere. At least for now."

Captain Vaughn nodded. "I convinced the king this was an isolated event. He fears the incident could give hope to the witchfolk that the shield witch urban legend is true. No one has survived a stoning in recent history but the legend persists."

"I'm not surprised. My brother fears looking weak. And if his quicksilver punishment no longer works...well, then there is nothing stopping the witchfolk from rising up. That's Elios' greatest fear."

"Then let's spread the word. Tell every witch about what we're doing here. Are we fighters or cowards? What is the point of Medusa' coven if we don't act? An uprising *should* scare him. Let's make the king's nightmares come true," Amber said.

While the mages prayed to Circe and vilified Medusa, the witchfolk worshipped Medusa. Made in her image, the witchfolk were the god-cursed souls who could shapeshift and wield magic. Their folklore hailed her a hero, mother, and protector. But the word-of-mouth stories lacked consistency in the details. The coven was named in her honor. They would dethrone the king in her name.

"Are you going to give protection wards to all of the witchfolk who rise up? What if a ward fails? What if they don't believe in the cause?" Imani asked. She leaned onto the table with both elbows. Her black hair fell over her shoulder like a waterfall. "Then what? One must always have a backup plan. Have you forgotten your lessons so soon?"

Imani was in teacher mode. There was no answer that would satisfy her. Memories from being put on the spot during potions lectures at the Guild Academy made her mouth turn dry. Amber didn't have an answer that wouldn't start a fight. This was the real world, not a classroom. Lives were at stake. Bigger risks needed to be taken.

"Why are you afraid of trying, mom?" Jasmine asked. Her voice trembled slightly. "Isn't this what we've been working towards? Ending the stonings?"

"It is." Imani cocked an eyebrow, a smirk lifting the side of her mouth. She tapped a slender cinnamon-colored finger on the table. "Do you have a plan other than 'spread the word'? How are you going to make people follow you? How are you going to convince them to risk their lives on the strength of a legend? Where is your proof?"

Imani leaned back in her chair, waiting for an answer. Jasmine's silence filled the room. Her cheeks flushed red.

"We need you, all of you, to be safe," Selene said.

"We *are* being safe. Rynn was followed by the hunters. She was trying to help," Amber said.

"I understand but that is why you are supposed to be working on understanding the spell, not running unsanctioned missions in the shadows of Witchtown. It's too dangerous. We need to remake the witchblade as soon as possible. Elios is getting more erratic. He's trying to get us to create a class focused on charmtek gems. Have you made any progress finding the Medusa cipher?"

"Sort of," Amber cleared her throat. "We know what doesn't work. And we know it isn't in the royal library. We've checked every book that is even remotely related to casting or Medusa. There's nothing there that helps."

Decoding the witchblade spell was harder than any academy assignment. The spell's ingredients were jumbled and interwoven with a folktale about the founding of the kingdom. They didn't know which items to choose or how to combine them safely. The other problem was that the story didn't match the official records. Officially, Circe was a goddess who founded the kingdom and Medusa was a witch, warmonger, and goddess-killer.

The spell book's story called Circe a goddess and a witch. She helped a cursed Medusa flee the god-realm to theirs through a portal. They brought the other beings cursed by the gods and created a haven for them on Belle Isle. There was no war between the women. There was no evil witch. Only love and respect. The witchfolk were survivors of the gods' wrath and vile amusements. The gods armed Perseus and the hunter Orion with quicksilver swords to trap Medusa and her kin in stone. Circe and Medusa crafted the witchblade spell to free the witchfolk from the quicksilver prison. Medusa killed Perseus and sent his head back to the god-realm.

"A line in the spell pointed us to the Skyfarmer's Almanac," Jasmine added. "We checked the Almanac but there are hundreds of ciphers listed in the index. None of them mention Medusa beyond the founding story."

"It doesn't help that each spell was encoded using a different cipher. The ciphers unlocked a few of the other spells but the witchblade spell is still just a glorified shopping list without the right code. We've tried everything," Amber said. "We need more time. It's only been a month."

"What about the puzzlebox?" Selene asked.

The puzzlebox was an even worse challenge than the spell. It was something straight out of a fairytale, a reverie. According to the stories, it could hold memory projections. In the fairytales it was used by forbidden lovers and spies alike. Made of glass and silver, the pill-shaped vault was half the length of her forearm and roughly equal to the thickness of her wrist. Nine movable rings wrapped around the puzzlebox like bracelets. Each ring displayed a set of engraved onyx letters.

None of her charms had cracked the seal on the vault. Jasmine even tried coaxing it open with a silvertongue spell to no avail. They used all the words from the folktale in the spellbook but there were too many possible combinations. Whatever was inside, the queen had valued highly. Maybe it was a map to the witchblade. Or maybe it was a memory of how to make the witchblade. But those were just guesses wrapped in hope. It could all be a wild goose chase. Amber had no clue what was inside.

"We thought the password might have something to do with the witching hour. The nine rings on the puzzlebox match the nine phases of the moon. And the witching hour is mentioned in the spell and some folktales about the witchblade. But *hollow moon* is too long for the password."

"Hmm." Selene drummed her fingers on the table. "And what of the boy, Vera's kinfolk?"

"Zerrick Reeve. We're meeting him today at the Lunchbox."

Allegedly, Zerrick's great-grandmother Vera was the only witch to be revived from the stonings by Queen Celeste. The family went into hiding after the queen was stoned by the king. It took two generations for them to resurface in the public record seven years ago. Amber found their name when searching the witchfolk registration files. The files listed information on all the witchfolk impacted by the dragon fever. The name was changed from Reeves to Reeve, but Amber knew it was the same family. She felt it in her bones. Rynn had risked and lost everything to find him. *This had to work.*

"You're sure you can trust him?"

"He's a monk. Everything we talk to him about will stay hidden. Besides, Rynn trusted him. That's enough for me."

"How fortunate," Tarkan said. He stroked his beard absentmindedly. The habit was the same one Kane did when he was thinking. "It seems goddess Circe is smiling on us."

"And if the boy refuses to help?" Imani asked.

"I'll take care of it," Jasmine said. "I've been practicing. I can get him to talk."

"Very well. One last thing. It's about your guild license. I'm sorry but it was denied. We found out on our way here." Selene slid a red and black envelope across the table.

"What? Why? How?" Amber sat forward. "Was it him? Was it the king?"

"Unofficially, no. But yes. The other guildmasters took a vote without me. Elios has been meeting in secret with Nevin and Clayton. This is just their latest betrayal. I don't know what they're up to, but I doubt it's good. I am sorry. We will fix it. Somehow. Don't worry dear. I'll talk to Elios."

Amber wasn't worried. She was pissed. She had to stop the king.

3

"Denied." Amber blinked. She read the letter again. The words didn't change. Her license was denied. Without it she was no better than a mundane. If she was caught using a wand without a license she'd be stoned. *All that time wasted at the academy.* She knew the king was trying to punish her for her mother's sins, but this was too much.

Amber huddled in a corner booth of the Lunchbox with Kane and Jasmine. Celebration for the foxhunt was in full swing in the diner. She checked her pocket watch; the opening ceremony was only a couple hours away. They didn't have much time to get this meeting done.

Their regular waitress came to the table. Marj set down three platters of food and three mugs of lavender lemonade with a nod. Amber smiled and thanked her. The smell of the hand pies made her stomach grumble. She hadn't realized she was hungry. She scooped up a hand pie and ate half in a single bite.

"Let me see." Jasmine took the letter and read it aloud, "Denial reason: Violation of the Kingslaw, rule fifty-six: *Applicant is an unmarried woman of marrying age.* Reapply with proof of marriage and your husband's signature as proof of his permission."

"Now I need to be married to join the guild. This can't be real." Amber let out a deep sigh. *Permission. What the hell was happening?*

"Why the change? Why now?" Kane asked.

"To take away the thing I want the most so I will marry who he wants." Amber took a long drink from her mug. The lavender lemonade tickled her tongue and warmed her belly. "Okay. So, he tried to arrange a marriage for me and my mom rejected it because I was only seventeen. But now that I'm old enough to get my license and get married he's found a way to control me and punish my mom for defying him."

She skipped telling them the whole truth. She was a pawn in the lifelong war between her mom and the king. According to her mom, during his first year on the throne, the king betrothed her to a lesser noble to secure an alliance. She broke off the arrangement and married Amber's dad instead. It was her uncle's first failure as king. He hated her mom for making him look weak. Now he was using her to punish her mom. Their sibling rivalry was going to kill her.

"Arrange a marriage to who?" Kane asked. "Why didn't you tell me?"

"She never told me who it was, so I figured it didn't matter. All the nobles want to join the royal family. It could be any one of them." Amber shrugged.

"I don't know if the nobles will stand for this. This law doesn't just control you. It's going to punish every woman who graduates from the academy. It would've impacted me if my birthday wasn't before graduation."

"They're too brainwashed to fight back. They won't question any law he passes as long as it's for the safety and wellness of the guild," Amber said. "Kingslaw protects them from the *scary* witches."

"Well, you need to figure something out before the king arranges another marriage for you," Kane said. "That is if you still want your wand."

"Well, you two could get married. The king wouldn't be able to stop you from getting your license then." Jasmine chuckled. "And he would keep your secret safe."

"Talk about abuse of power." Amber laughed off the awkward moment. "I'm being forced into marriage, so I force my guard to marry me. Yeah, no. We'll remake the witchblade and take down the king before I have to worry about marriage. I have time."

Amber didn't want Kane to know how she felt. It would kill her to hear him say what she already knew, he didn't love her back. They were merely stuck together by royal duty. His family had protected hers for one hundred years. He'd been raised to be her sworn protector because of that history. His dad served as her mom's personal royal guard. Despite her mom being one of the strongest mages in the guild, Tarkan stayed at her mom's side nearly as much as Kane stayed at hers. Amber knew her feelings would fade over time, she just had to wait them out and keep it secret until then.

"Whatever you need, princess," Kane said. "As long as you're safe, my job's done."

"See." Jasmine smiled and winked at her. "Problem solved. Call me team Kamber."

"*Anyway*, Zerrick is over an hour late." Amber turned her attention to the door. "Are we sure he's coming?"

"Rynn found him. She gave him the info. He'll show," Kane said.

"What if he heard about what happened to her? I mean, I wouldn't show up after that. Would you?"

"I don't know. Maybe." Kane shook his head.

The possibility hung between them. *Dammit*. Her need to protect Rynn could've cost them the chance to protect everyone. The waitress came back to their table with a tray on one hip. The copper clockwork gears in her arm glowed orange as she set a pitcher of lavender lemonade down. She refilled their drinks with a tap of her wand, draining the liquid from the pitcher into their cups.

"Any dessert today?" she asked. "We have blackberry cookies and apple fritters fresh from Sinclaire's."

"A basket of each, please," Amber said.

"A note. From your friend." Marj handed her a square piece of paper from atop the stack of napkins on the tray.

"Thanks, Marj. I owe you one." Amber took the note. The paper was written in witch ink. Another charm. It was invisible to

14

non-witchfolk and unreadable to those untrained in the witch language. Amber studied the paper. The green ink shimmered in the light. *What in the fresh hells?* Amber crumpled up the paper and tossed it onto her platter. She snapped her fingers. The paper ball ignited in a green flash, leaving behind a small pile of white ash.

"What'd it say?" Jasmine asked.

"Meet me at the prayer rooms in the green temple." Amber answered.

"Great. He's changing the plans. Are you sure this what you want to do?" Kane asked.

"You think it's a trap?"

He stroked his goatee before he answered. A shadow fell over his face, his thoughts turning inward.

"It should be fine. Not ideal but if we run into any trouble just follow my lead. Don't do anything rash. Stay in disguise. We don't know how much we can trust him yet."

"I'll be on best behavior." Amber held up a hand. "Royal's honor."

4

Amber's pulse raced as they walked through the massive emerald door of the green temple. She hadn't been to temple in seven years. Not since the dragon fever spread through the city like wildfire. Any god who allowed witchfolk to lose their powers was no different than the devilish men who took them. And neither was worthy of worship. The temple was nearly empty, maybe she wasn't the only one who felt that way. As they walked through the hallways the green marble floors and walls surrounded them like a forest. The double crescent hollow moon symbol of the goddess Circe decorated the walls in a looping pattern. Onyx statues of Circe encircled the massive ivory columns that dotted the hallway.

"It's creepy in here." Jasmine scratched at her neck.

"Stop. You'll break the charm." Amber pulled Jasmine's hand away.

"Sorry. My guild sigil is itchy."

Covering their sigils was the hardest part of cloaking them in disguises. Stacking charms was hard, uncomfortable, and potentially deadly if done wrong. Amber could shift their appearances with a touch despite the cloaking charm on her wrist that hid her witch blood from detection. However, the guild sigils fought back against her charms. That was where Kane came into play. He was one of the best menders in the kingdom. Amber often wished she had his healing powers, but she didn't have the patience for the training to become a mender.

Kane placed a hand on Jasmine's arm. "Better?"

"Much. Thanks!" Jasmine rolled her neck in a circle.

Amber led the way to the prayer rooms. The rental desk was monitored by a silent monk. Her head was clean shaven, her mouth tongueless. Emerald jewelry adorned her forehead in a mix of piercings that formed the symbol of the goddess. Amber provided her fake name in exchange for the key to the new moon room.

Kane opened the door, taking the lead in entering the room. Amber followed Jasmine inside. The smell of roasting pinecones and vanilla hit her like a punch to the ribs. The room was sparsely decorated. At the far end of the room a simple altar was set up with an incense burner, lit candle, and black offering candles. It was decorated with a garland of pink Aphrodite's Promise. A copy of the Skyfarmer's Almanac was propped up on the edge of the table. The ornate cover was engraved in gold with the nine phases of the moon. Amber didn't understand the nuances of the religion. It was confusing why the kingdom hated witchfolk but used a book that displayed the hollow moon symbol of the witching hour on its favorite book. As the kingdom's official religious and history book, the Almanac stored both prayers and prophecies as well as the Kingslaw, spells, maps, and statistics. Amber hoped this monk knew it well.

Zerrick stood in the middle of the room with his back to them. He was dressed in a deep green vest with black trousers, the quicksilver binding cuffs glistened around his wrists. When he turned around Jasmine let out a quiet gasp. Rynn had failed to mention that Zerrick was gorgeous. Not as much as Kane but still, he was a close second. He was half a head taller than Kane with a similar tawny complexion. He had broad shoulders and muscular arms that looked like they were carved by Circe herself. His chestnut eyes were framed by a nearly flawless face. His nose was slightly crooked as if it had been broken and set improperly. A black and green symbol of the goddess decorated his right arm from shoulder to elbow. As it shimmered against his skin, Amber wondered if it was decoration or something more.

"Rynn said you needed info." He crossed his arms. "Ask."

"Tell us about Vera Reeves or Reeve. We need to know how she was cured," Kane said.

Zerrick took a deep breath. "A witchblade."

"We know that. Everyone knows that. We need to know how. What happened to Vera after. Where is the witchblade?" The words rushed out of Amber. "This is life or death."

"Is it? Oh. I had no idea." Zerrrick laughed. "You think you are the first to try to find or remake it? Good luck. Don't die trying."

Jasmine took a step forward. She was their best weapon on this mission. If Zerrick knew anything, her siren power would pull it out of him.

"Tell the truth. *Veritas dico*," Jasmine whispered. The silvertongue charm tattooed inside her bottom lip did its job. Her words curled out towards him in a trail of green smoke. The smoke stopped a handspan from Zerrick's ear as if they hit a brick wall.

"Really?" Zerrick tilted his head to the side and cocked an eyebrow at her. He tapped the tattoo on his arm. "Protection ward. I'm in the order of sin eaters. A guardian of secrets. Want to try again? Or should we just call it a day?" Zerrick took a step toward the door.

Jasmine shot a look to Amber. She shrugged. Time for a different approach. Amber touched Jasmine's arm, letting the disguise fall away. Zerrick's face softened as his eyes scanned Jasmine in her true form.

"I'm Jasmine, heir to the air guild. We need your help. I know Rynn is your friend. She was taken this morning for breaking the witching hour curfew. Her stoning failed due to a protection ward. The axman was killed in the process." Jasmine held up a hand to stop Zerrick from interrupting. "She's safe for now but we don't know how long that will last. We *need* the witchblade. Breaking the curse is our only chance at saving her. At saving everyone. Please. Anything you know could help. Any detail you think isn't important, it could be a game changer."

Zerrick sighed. He ran a hand over his shaved head. "Shit. I don't know."

Amber touched Kane's arm and dropped her own disguise at the same time.

"Princess?" Zerrick stared at her royal sigil. "But...you're a witch. I'd heard rumors there were unregistered witchfolk passing as mages in the guilds but a royal? I thought that was just an urban legend. This can't be real. Can it?"

"It is and I am. Another secret I'll ask you to keep. And it's just Amber. We're running short on time. We have Queen Celeste's spellbook written in witch ink. Every cipher we try leads us to dead ends. We need to find the right cipher to crack the code. We think the key is the Almanac, but we don't know where to start. *Anything* you know about Vera could help," Amber said. "Please."

"I only know the story my mom told. It's the same story that witchfolk whispered in the shadows. Vera was my mom's grandmother. She was a witch, monk, and friend of the queen." Zerrick recited the words as if he'd said them a hundred times before. "Vera gave advice to the queen about King Wesley. That advice got Vera stoned. The queen woke her up with a kiss of the witchblade during the witching hour. She gave Vera the witchblade to hide. The next morning, King Wesley named the queen a traitor and stoned her. The royal guard locked down Witchtown and searched for Vera. She was never found. The blade was lost with her." Zerrick shrugged. "My grandma and mom had to hide for a while and then they didn't. That's it."

"She was a monk?" Amber paced across the room. "I've never heard that before."

"Well, she was. My mom turned her back on the temple after I was born. She didn't trust any of it after they went into hiding. If it wasn't for my dad getting sick with the dragon fever, she'd probably still be on the run."

"I'm so sorry for your loss." Jasmine touched his elbow.

"Thank you. That's what pushed me to join the temple. I volunteered at the temple when the fever was spreading. The monkhood gave me a purpose. A way to help."

"You called yourself a guardian of secrets. What does that mean, *exactly*?"

"We take confessions. We eat sins. We protect them with our lives. The promises are etched on our bodies." Zerrick turned his back to them. In a quick motion he took off his vest revealing a bare back covered in a black and green honeycomb pattern.

"So, you don't give advice?" Kane asked.

"Giving advice is forbidden." Zerrick shrugged his vest back on then turned to face them.

"Then the legend is wrong. Vera took the queen's secret. She didn't give her advice. Maybe she gave her something else. Like a cipher." Amber glanced at the altar. "Can you think of any secret or hidden ciphers? Something not listed in the index."

"The Skyfarmer's Almanac takes a lifetime to fully understand. The versions change every year. Sometimes twice a year depending on the seers' visions. If you don't know what volume to use, it's useless." Zerrick rubbed his head again. "I wouldn't know where to start."

"We start in the guild library," Jasmine said. "It's the only official library. It has every volume of the Almanac. If the answer is in there, we'll find it."

"And you want to go now?"

"We're going to sneak out of the foxhunt once they start. Kane's dad is going to take up watch of the royal box himself and the library should be nearly empty. That way we'll have less chance of any unwanted onlookers while we work," Amber said.

"I hate to ask but if you aren't registered, how are you able to bypass the library security system?"

"Cloaking charm." Amber held out her left wrist. "My dad hid it under my royal mark when I was a baby. The charm acts as a cage. My familiar spirit fights against it whenever I get excited. I can still shift but it hurts like hell. I've gotten used to it over the years."

"You mean angry," Kane said.

"Whatever. The point is it works. Are you in?"

"If it helps Rynn and the other witchfolk, I'm in." Zerrick nodded.

"Okay, now we hurry up and wait," Amber sighed.

5

Amber was in no mood for bloodsport. Her thoughts raced from decoding the spellbook to Rynn's fate in jail to the denial of her license. The urge to keep moving coursed through her body. She paced the span of the royal box. Her familiar clawed at her chest. Her temples throbbed to the same tempo as her temples. There was no calming it.

"Breathe," Kane said from his seat at the front of the box.

Amber grunted dismissively.

"Eat something."

Another grunt.

"Princess, please. We're stuck here for now. Just sit and wait. It won't be long."

He was right. With a deep breath she grabbed a sandwich off the snack table then joined him. Looking down at the arena spiked her heartbeat. She wasn't the biggest fan of heights. As the top row in the arena, the royal box nearly touched the ceiling. The distance from the labyrinth made her dizzy.

The arena vibrated with chatter and cheers over the deep thrum of drums played by the orchestra. The flatscreens in the royal box gave her a closeup view of the arena from her bird's eye perch. The labyrinth at the center of the square arena floor descended two stories under the stadium. Four orange gems glowed at the corners of the labyrinth's ceiling. They formed an invisible barrier that blocked magical interference from the crowd. The wards were an unnecessary precaution. Only guards and the royals were allowed to have their wands in the arena during foxhunt. Between gambling and guild pride, it was too dangerous to have that many armed mages in the same room at once.

The labyrinth was a simple maze design, lacking any dead ends. One twisting path led to the prize in the center. There was one way in and one way out. Despite the wall sconces emitting white light, the black marble walls cast unnatural shadows at the corners of pathway. A round stage floated above the sunken labyrinth. Upon it sat the guildmasters and the royal family, and the most recent champion.

Although there was no official seating arrangement, the guilds self-segregated into three distinct groups around the arena. The fire section was situated under the royal box in a sea of red and black uniforms. The fire mages held banners and wore vests emblazoned with red and black dragons. Amber marveled at how the mascot's eyes glowed like red hot coals. The bottom level held the stage for the orchestra and special seating for the guildmasters and the royal family once the foxhunt began.

Looking counterclockwise around the arena a clash of colors met her gaze. To her left, the water mages were decked out in teal unicorn horn hats. Across from her, the air mages flew shimmering lavender and grey paper kites in the shape of their mascot, a griffin in flight. To her right, a small group of mundanes and cuffed witchfolk sat in a sea of white. Although they couldn't join the guild, a few won lottery tickets to attend the foxhunt. They were required to wear white vests so they could be easily identified. Rynn said that when she first attended the labyrinth the battles had broken her heart and inspired her, the same mixed up feelings Amber had. Despite the horrors the witchfolk faced in the labyrinth, this was the only time they could fully shift. Freed of the quicksilver cuffs, they were fitted with charmtek shock collars. Neither cage was fair.

Before Kingrise, there was a fourth guild – earth. Founded and populated by witchfolk, earth was the first guild. witchfolk didn't have to study or use wands to tap into their magic. For ages, there was harmony amongst the witchfolk and mages to whom they taught the craft. But Kingrise ushered in an age of ignorance and suffering fueled by the king's paranoia. Following an alleged failed assassination attempt by his witch wife, he destroyed what the witchfolk had created. The earth guild was banned, its members arrested, killed, or sent into hiding. The king required all the folk to wear binding cuffs that stopped them from shifting into their familiar. The cursed cuffs were designed to take away their dangerousness but not their usefulness. Although dampened, witchfolk could still tap into aura to do basic crafting of rock and earth. This made them the perfect workhorses for the crown. They were forced to work in the royal mines, fields, and army. If they misused their powers, they were forced to watch their families stoned before facing the same fate.

Her heart beat in a syncopated rhythm with an ache for all that was lost. She hated seeing her own kind mistreated. A lifetime of watching the atrocities while caging her true nature, created a barely controlled rage in her soul. As a crownless royal, Amber was granted more freedom than if she were in line for the crown. However, attending the foxhunt was part of her royal duties, crown or not. She hated the foxhunt. The monthly event only reinforced the divisions between the guilds, pitting them against each other for bragging rights and a symbol of evil: a quicksilver dagger.

The royal box was another cage. Her mom refused to let her sit in the stands with the fire guild after she almost shifted into her familiar when she was thirteen. Her powers were newly gained, and she was still learning to control them. Admittedly, Amber had bared her fangs at a mundane but it wasn't her fault. The fool had tried to sell her a charm made of unicorn horn. Her mom wiped his memory but that wasn't enough. Amber understood her mom's fear, but it still pissed her off. She couldn't even have Jasmine in the royal box as a guest. She was all alone with Kane and his unusually foul mood. She wasn't sure which of them hated the foxhunt more. Maybe he just hated the reminder of his loss last year.

"There goes the champ." Sarcasm dripped from Kane's words.

Amber switched her attention to the screen as the announcer's voice echoed through the arena.

"Seven-time champion, Gavin Wade, the Butcher."

Thunderous applause shook the walls. Gavin stood at the center of the stage. He wore a white vest over his grey hunter's uniform. The hilts of his quicksilver daggers shone in his shoulder holster. He waved to the crowd with a woodenness that matched the mask-like grin plastered on his face. Amber hated that they let him come back after he was kicked out the guild last month. He had no business being put in the spotlight after almost killing another mage. It didn't matter how many wins he had.

"Jealous, much?" Amber poked him in the rib cage. She hoped his mood would brighten with a little trash talk.

"The day I'm jealous of Gavin, is the day I'll quit the guild and join the monkhood."

"So, you're saying you'd abandon me? That hurts."

"Never."

"I'm surprised he's here after this morning."

"I'm not. He'd never miss an opportunity to be in the spotlight. Doesn't help that half the guild has been treating him like a god since his last win."

"Yeah well, people are dumb." Amber shrugged. "You should have won."

"Doesn't matter." Kane scoffed. He cocked his head towards the stage. "The guildmasters have their own agenda. They want the bloodshed."

"Okay but attacking another mage to win is just wrong. If you hadn't stopped to save Bowen, he would've died."

"Wrong or not Gavin technically didn't break the rules. They care about the spectacle and Gavin delivered."

The orchestra played the guild anthem softly.

"Here we go," Amber said.

The announcer's voice blazed through the arena, introducing each of the guildmasters in turn as they stood up from their thrones to wave at the crowd.

"Fire guildmaster, crownless princess Selene Silverby. The Firekeeper."

Her mother stood in front of the middle throne. Behind her, a banner with glowing dragon eyes fluttered softly. She wore an off-the-shoulder floor length black gown. Her corset was embroidered with a red dragon in flight. Her hair hung loose around her face in golden curls that bounced when she waved. Her grey eyes looked like ash from a long dead fire.

"Air guildmaster Clayton Overton. The Stormchaser," the announcer said.

Jasmine's dad waved to the crowd as he stood in front of his throne. His lavender suit clung to his arms and legs. It gave the impression of a wind-caught sail. His bright smile and umber complexion were the same as Jasmine's after she tanned in the summer.

"Water guildmaster, Nevin Wade. The Shipbreaker."

He wore black slacks with matching vest over a teal dress shirt that bulged against his biceps. With his pale skin, greasy hair, and large ears, he was the spitting image of his son, Gavin.

Every year she had watched the foxhunt as a royal, and then as a fire guild member. Now she watched as a conspirator and enemy of the crown. If her mission was successful, by the time the foxhunt ended the witching hour would dawn and the king would fall. But first she needed the witchblade to break the quicksilver curse.

Seated at center stage was the royal family. The king sat in the tallest throne on the stage. His golden crown sparkled with sapphires that flattered his blonde hair and blue eyes. He wore the ceremonial dress uniform, including two leg holsters, one for his dagger, the other for his wand. The same as her uniform. A copper clockwork necklace with four orange gems hung around his neck. It looked like an oversized shirt button. The king adjusted his crown reflexively to cover the missing tip of his ear. A red scar trailed the side of his cheek to his chin. A gift from her mom. Based on her own experience, Amber knew the king didn't know how to use either the dagger or wand well when it really mattered. He was lazy, relying on his guards to save him before he saved himself. When he was cornered, he was no match for a real fight.

Her twin cousins Maximo and Nazim sat in thrones flanking the widower king. They were identical, the spitting image of the king with blue eyes and pale skin. As crown prince, Maximo's uniform matched the king's with the exception of the crown. Maximo's was smaller and adorned with rubies. Nazim wore a white vest over his ash grey witch hunter uniform and a scowl that matched the sharpness of the twin blades holstered on his hips. A faint orange glow surrounded the ring on his right hand. Truly his father's son.

A crescendo from the orchestra's strings section cut through the air. All noise in the arena stopped as the king stood. He walked to the middle of the stage to his own syncopated royal anthem, the Crown's March. The sound sent goosebumps up her arms.

"King Elios, the Tinkerer," the announcer said.

"Happy Foxhunt Day! Today we celebrate King Wesley the Divine. One hundred years ago my grandfather survived an assassination attempt orchestrated by his witch wife, the witch queen Celeste. When King Wesley took the throne, he ushered in a new era of harmony for our country. Before his reign our country was barely distinct from the American wastelands. Unholy witches roamed freely in our streets plotting against good mages. Our guilds were weak with infighting and jealousy. Our American enemies laughed at our shortcomings.

"Now, thanks to charmtek, we are a kingdom of innovation and industry, better than any mundane's dreams. Now, our witches are cuffed and controlled. Now our guilds are filled with the strongest fighters in the world. Our enemies no longer laugh. We are the blueprint for greatness. As Michigan goes, so goes the world."

"So goes the world!" The crowd answered in unison.

"We host the foxhunt in honor of King Wesley as celebration of his life and remembrance of his noble death. It was on a foxhunt that he lost his life protecting his daughter, my mother Queen Dawn the Protector, from a witch attack. The mages battle witches in his honor, completing the foxhunt that he couldn't. It is within these battles we find our strongest mages. And with strong mages, we strengthen the kingdom." He cleared his throat. "Now, I'm pleased to announce an alliance that will further strengthen our homeland."

Gavin took three steps forward. Amber's stomach tightened. Kane stiffened next to her.

"Our beloved champion, Gavin Wade, witch hunter extraordinaire has asked for my niece's hand in marriage. Although Amber is crownless, the allegiance between our families is ideal. The wedding is to take place before the closing ceremony of the foxhunt. Now, I hand things over to the monk to bless this celebration."

"God fortify the king." The monk greeted the crowd with a ceremonial bow. "May the goddess Circe smile on you all. Tod—"

Amber didn't hear the monk's prayer. Her focus was on not torching the place. She could control her emotions and not shift into her familiar in most situations. But this... *Breathe in. Breathe out.* The arena disappeared around her. There was only the bright red rage flowing from her core to her fingertips. *Breathe in. Breathe out.* Not now. Not like this.

Kane put a calming hand on her shoulder.

"Signal Jasmine. We need to talk." Amber refocused.

WITCHFOLK

First Rynn then her license and now this. She stared at the king and his shit-eating grin. Someone needed to wipe it off his face, permanently. *Breathe in. Breathe out.*

6

Kane wrote a sigil on the door frame of the closet. When she stepped through the door, the room was much larger than it had been before. He'd become a master at the hideaway spaces since they discovered the spells in Queen Celeste's spellbook a few months ago. The hideaways were the key to their secret coven meetings. Write a modifier sigil on a door, transform a room. Write a portal sigil and the door opened to another part of the kingdom. The charms warded off all sound and were invisible. They were great for quick escapes and secret sharing. Amber was less skilled at the charms but could pull off a basic hideaway if needed.

"What game is the king playing?" Amber paced back and forth. The rhythmic clicking of her heels on the marble floors calmed her nerves. She ran through the likely scenarios, muttering as she weighed the possibilities. "This is why he put the new guild license rule in place. They think they can force me to marry Gavin. But why? To make Gavin a royal? To get something from me?" *What the hell were they up to?*

"Maybe the king owes a debt. Gavin's father has his hands in a lot of pockets in the kingdom." Kane leaned against the wall in their makeshift meeting room. His hands rested on the hilts of his daggers. "Or he's rewarding Gavin for winning the foxhunt." He shrugged. "Either wa—"

"So, I'm a prize? Or a favor?"

"Or a threat." Kane took a step toward her. "Maybe he told the king."

"Shit." Amber exhaled deeply. "What do we do? I can't marry him."

"Hide?"

"Too hard."

"Stone him?"

"Too obvious."

"Kill him?"

"Too risky."

"I could threaten him." Kane absentmindedly tossed one of his daggers end-over-end, catching the hilt effortlessly.

"Too...easy. Then you'd get in trouble again. No. It has to be someth—"

A small vibration buzzed her thumb ring. Jasmine. The spy rings were another charm from the queen. The matching gold rings were crafted with a charm of conspiracy. It had taken a while to get the engravings on the spy rings right. Eventually they figured out how to stay in contact even from opposite ends of the kingdom. It was a more secure system than the mundane phones that were easily hacked with an eavesdrop charm.

Kane opened the door to let Jasmine and Zerrick slip inside the room. Jasmine made a beeline to Amber and wrapped her in a tight hug.

"You okay?" Jasmine held her by the shoulders at arm's length. "I can't believe..."

"I know. It's a nightmare."

"Do you think the king knows?" Jasmine folded her arms across her chest.

"Maybe. No. I don't know. What am I going to do? I can't..." Amber's voice cracked. Tears pressed at the back of her eyes. "He hunts witches. If he w—"

"You could take the monk's vow." Zerrick offered.

They all turned in unison to face him. Of course a monk would suggest that.

"Joining the temple is another trap." Jasmine shook her head. "But another vow might work."

"You can't be serious." Amber took a step back.

"It's Kingslaw. Marriage outlasts death. That's how Wesley took and kept the throne from Celeste," Jasmine said.

A thought sent goosebumps up her arms. "Maybe he kept my secret so he could use me. Gavin wants to rejoin the guild. He's going to use the marriage right to join fire guild."

Most people spent a lifetime focused on joining one guild. Mastery of one element took a lifetime. A select few attempted to join multiple guilds. Even fewer were successful. It wasn't prohibited outright but it was frowned upon. The guilds were protective of their secrets. And the entrance exams and fees for multiple memberships supported the unofficial prohibition. There was one exception, the marriage right. Under Kingslaw, spouses were free to join the guild of their spouse to preserve trust in the marriage and protect guild secrets.

"Shit. You're right," Jasmine said.

"The king wants a marriage. Let's give him one," Kane said. "If you'll have me."

"But I can't ask you to do that."

"I think I just asked you, actually." He smiled.

"I-I...there has to be another way..."

"Amber, it seems like this is the only way. The king made sure of that with his speech. You can't outright reject the marriage proposal without backlash, and the king can't defy Kingslaw. He'll have to respect the marriage." Jasmine forced a smile. "And they'll have to give you your guild license. That's a big win."

"And mom would approve. I mean she did it herself." Amber added. Her words did little to calm the panic in her chest. She turned her attention fully to Kane. "You're okay with this?"

"Whatever you need, princess. I'm here, always."

"Okay, then. The library will wait." Amber turned to Zerrick, "How do we do this?"

7

Amber paced as her watch ticked away the minutes. They had a small window of time to execute their plan. Once the opening ceremony ended, her absence would be noticed. Tradition required the royal family to greet the contenders as they entered the labyrinth. They bestowed good luck on the contenders in the form of bloodred daisies. It was a trivial part of the foxhunt but if she wasn't there to hand out her flowers it would be a problem.

Jasmine, Zerrick, and Kane hadn't returned from the temple yet. *How long was long enough to start to worry?* They'd left her alone in the hideaway. An anchor point for them to reconvene and complete the wedding ceremony. Jasmine was helping Zerrick gather the holy ceremonial items while Kane provided the hideaway charms. She would have preferred they all stayed together but there was no time. They couldn't do the ceremony in the temple for fear of getting caught. But waiting for them to return put a different fear in her heart. What if they failed? As she started to spiral with more fatalistic questions, the door opened. Amber's stomach unclenched. Alright. Everything was going to be alright.

"Are you all okay?" Amber asked. "That took longer than you said."

"Sorry. We had to be careful grabbing your guild papers from your room. There were more guards around than I thought," Jasmine said.

"And there were guards doing rounds in the temple. They almost never set foot inside," Zerrick said.

"They must be on alert from Rynn's stoning. That's my fault," Amber apologized.

"But we have everything we need." Zerrick held up his satchel as proof. "Ribbon, Aphrodite's Promise, and stardust wine."

"Thank you. What do you need from us?" Amber asked.

"Repeat the prayer charm, eat the petal, drink the wine. And it's done."

"Can we have a minute?" Amber asked as she pulled Kane to the side of the room by the hand. "Are you sure about this? You don't have to. It's a big deal. Tell me now and I'll find another way to avoid Gavin."

"We were already stuck together, princess. Might as well have fun and give 'em hell while we can. Imagine the look on Gavin's face when he finds out." He chuckled. "This is the best payback for that bonehead."

Amber was looking forward to seeing the king's face when she gave him the news. Gavin hadn't crossed her mind. But he would undoubtedly be put out that his rival was marrying the princess he wanted. Afterall, Gavin was a collector. He traipsed around the kingdom and the outer lands hunting witchfolk. She'd heard tell of his trophy case. All of which she believed and none of which she wished to see. *I refuse to be added to his collection, neither as his bride nor as his prey.*

"We're ready."

Zerrick walked them through the ceremony like a seasoned pro. Though he said the process was simple, it was detailed. First, he had them hold hands while he read a ceremonial prayer from the Skyfarmer's Almanac. Next, he wrapped the ribbon around their intertwined left hands three times, in exaggerated loops. They both chuckled as the ribbon billowed between them like a lost kite. They straightened up after a stern look from Jasmine.

"The ceremonial ribbon has been placed. It is time for your vows." Zerrick dropped his hand as if signaling the start of a race.

Amber stifled another chuckle. They followed the directions he gave them. Together they plucked a pink and blue heart-shaped petal from the Aphrodite's Promise plant. They each took half the petal and fed it to each other. Kane said the vow first.

"I'm yours, always." He took a sip from the glass that drained half the stardust wine.

Amber took the glass from him, said the same vow, then emptied the glass. The wine tasted of honey, strawberries, and pepper. Not as good as lavender lemonade but the kick was stronger. The memory of eating strawberries while counting the stars and holding hands came back to her. She looked at Kane, his eyes locked into hers. *Did he remember too?* A searing cold pain flashed on her left hand. A black infinity heart symbol was etched on her middle finger. The marriage mark. Kane held out his hand to show a matching mark. *That was one helluva vow.*

"I now proclaim you as husband and wife. May the goddess smile on you."

"May the goddess smile on you, too." Amber and Kane repeated the blessing in unison.

"So, that's done," Jasmine said. "Good job, Zerrick. Now, what? Back to the arena? I really don't want to watch the foxhunt."

"Not yet. We have one stop to make first." Amber turned to Kane. "Husband? Ready to perform your first husbandly duty?"

"For you, anything." Kane smirked. "If you ask nicely, *wife.*"

"Will you pretty please give me your permission to join the guild and play with fire?"

"As long as you don't burn the kingdom down."

"No promises."

"You two are the most unserious people I know." Jasmine shook her head.

"Aww. Are you quitting team Kamber already?" Amber elbowed her teasingly.

"Keep acting up and find out."

"Fiesty." Amber hooked her elbow around Jasmine's and led the way through the portal.

8

Despite the holiday, the guild office was open. Her mouth dried at the sight of the "**NO WITCHES ALLOWED**" sign posted next to the door. Memories flooded back to her. When they were thirteen, she snuck out nightly with Jasmine to burn signs that were posted across the city. She set lots of fires back then, it was her only way of fighting back against the hateful mages and mundanes. They were younger then, more impulsive. The fires made them feel more in control, but it was all child's play. It wasn't actually fixing the problem. They'd graduated from those acts of vandalism to leading the resistance movement.

She followed Kane through the revolving door into the stark white marble and glass lobby. Three windows were cut into the wall directly across from the entrance. Over each was a banner for the respective guild it served. To the right of the desks was a secondary pair of windows cut into the thick marble wall. A sign hung between them. One arrow pointing left for dues, another to the right for licensing. A pair of older guards stood to the left, their eyes lazily scanned the lobby, and the few people scattered within it. Amber nodded to the pair of windows before she made her way over.

Behind the licensing window, a clerk dressed in a black uniform greeted them without looking up from her book.

"Happy Foxhunt Day. Welcome to the guild. Please place your license application, ID, and fee in the drop box." She pointed to a metal slot in the center of the windows as she spoke.

"Happy Foxhunt Day." Amber followed the directions. The clerk grabbed her paperwork from the drop box. Her neck snapped up when she looked at Amber's ID. Her eyes went from the ID to Amber's face a couple times before she spoke again.

"P-princess Silverby. Hello. Sorry. I-I didn't know it was you." She scrambled to stand and bow.

"Please, don't. It's just Amber." Amber read the name written on the clerk's nametag. "Sorry you can't enjoy the foxhunt, Willa."

"Oh no it's fine. I need the hours. Well, let me see about getting this processed for you." She flipped through the documents checking the information.

"And your husband, Kane Vaughn, he's here too?" The clerk asked.

"He is." Kane answered. He raised a hand to identify himself.

"Excellent. Excellent. And you give your permission freely?"

"I do."

"Excellent. Forgive me princess, but there seems to be an extra application in here. One for the water guild."

"No. Not extra. I need my license for the water guild as well. My *husband's* guild, with his permission of course."

"Of course. The marriage right." Recognition dawned on the clerk's face as she read the application. "Sorry, I don't get this type of application often. And your husband will be joining your guild."

"Indeed." Amber was cashing in on a rarely used ancient rule.

The clerk stamped the application then slid Amber's ID and new license through the drop box. Amber clutched the dual license with a sweaty palm. Gavin would have to put in the work to get into fire guild. No backroom deal was going to grant him the guild's secrets on her watch. She didn't know what he was searching for, but witch hunters never did anything that wasn't vile.

"You can take your licenses to the Inkmasters for your new guild sigils."

"The crown thanks you, Willa."

"And I thank the crown. And if I may say so, *good for you.*" Willa winked before dropping her eyes back to her book.

9

By chance or by design Amber was stuck standing next to Gavin. He reeked of fish and onions. Any appetite she had built up earlier disappeared within seconds of standing by his side. Amber completed her duties on the flower procession line in a daze. There were twice as many contestants compared to last month's foxhunt. She hazarded a guess that the increase in participation was due to the anniversary of Kingrise. The prestigious right to be named King's champion was pushed heavily in the guilds. It was the ultimate mark of success. To win on the anniversary was whole different level of prestige.

While the contestants filed past them, Amber kept her eyes forward. She felt Gavin staring at her. She made the mistake of looking in his direction when the line first started. The hungry look in his eyes reminded her of a cat on the hunt. Maybe he knew her secret. She pushed the thought aside. It didn't matter now. She had to focus on keeping herself calm for the upcoming confrontation with the king. He was definitely not going to be team Kamber.

She walked through numerous scenarios. None of them ended well. In every instance, there was pain. It wouldn't be immediate. Not for a coward like him. He'd pass out his punishments later, in unforeseen ways. She'd started a war with the king. No, he started the war years ago. She was going to finish it. She had no doubt that facing the king's wrath was far better than facing Gavin's cruelty.

The thoughts tumbled around in her mind until the procession ended. She hurried away from Gavin before he could speak to her. She didn't trust herself to not lash out if he said something hateful.

It was time for the next part of the foxhunt, midnight dinner. It technically started at sundown and lasted *until* midnight when dessert was served. The dinner symbolized what would be the last meal for many of the contestants. Dessert was a symbol of the kingdom's continued generosity. To honor the king, dessert was served at the arena during a clockwork play celebrating the founding of the kingdom. The crown provided free food and drinks to select eateries throughout the kingdom. They also paid entertainers for keeping the masses fed and drunk during the bloodbath of the foxhunt.

Traditionally, the royals feasted on midnight dinner at Honeypepper Lodge. It was centrally located near the arena. The eatery was the most exclusive in the city. It only served monks, nobles, and royals. Not even high-ranking guild members or royal guards could dine there without royal permission. It was all hype to preserve an air of superiority. The food was bland, the owner smug, and the staff abused. Amber hated the place. Every year she tried to get her mom to change the venue but there was no changing tradition in the king's mind. It was the lodge or nothing.

Per tradition, they traveled in a procession to the lodge. The fleet of clockwork driven skycabs were one of her least favorite parts of the day. The journey took mere minutes but left Amber with a new level of unease in her belly. She'd never been good with heights. Even less so when she was risking her life using glitchy magic. Charmtek was a joke. The only safe way for non-witchfolk to cast was using wands and spells. There was no official explanation of what powered the charmtek gems that didn't sound like a fairytale. Allegedly the gems harnessed goddess Circe's breath. Elios called it ether. It was a bullshit explanation. Amber suspected he was using some sort of dark magic to fuel the gems. If the gems had aura, she couldn't sense it.

Regardless of what fueled charmtek, it was unsafe and unstable. The glitches and accidents it caused were spreading through the city. Yet the king still pushed its use. The king was obsessed with using the copper machines as often as possible. It started with the mechanical butlers. Then it was clockwork drivers. Now it was the image projectors and flatscreens. It was too much change too fast. He claimed the charmtek showed the strength and innovation of the kingdom. Amber didn't care about any of that. She cared about not falling to her death if one of the charmtek powered tinker toys glitched.

The lodge was half-full when they arrived. The royals and nobles milled through the lodge, picking off the buffet and dabbling in conversation as bland as the food. Music drifted from the stage through the room. It was barely noticeable over the boisterous crowd. Kane found them a place near a corner to watch the party, away from prying eyes and groping hands. Clockwork butlers circled the room with trays of finger foods that looked less bland than the buffet offerings. But before Amber could get a drink or cheese wedge, her mother pulled her into a dark corner near the back of the room.

"How are you holding up? Are you practicing your breathing? I promise you, I didn't know about Elios' announcement. I would've put a stop to it." Selene sighed. She reached out and tucked a wavy strand of copper hair behind Amber's ear. "Today has been full of things out of my control apparently. I keep getting blindsided."

"I'm good. I'm in control, mom. Don't worry. I won't slip into my familiar." Amber smiled weakly. "You know that story you told me about your betrothal and dad?"

"Yes?"

"Well, what if I told you tha—"

"You didn't! You did. I should've never told you that story. I just didn't think it would ever matter. And now." Selene rubbed her forehead. "Who wa—"

"It was Kane. You understand though right? You aren't mad?"

"No, I'm not mad. I understand. Truly. And your license, did you secure that?"

"Yes. For fire *and* water."

"Kingslaw. Brilliant. That's my girl."

"Mom, why Gavin? Is it because he's a witch hunter or do you think they know about this morning?"

"I doubt it. If they knew you were behind anything, Elios would've sent the whole of the guard to arrest you just to spite me. No. I have my suspicions Gavin just wants back into the guild. Nevin pitched a fit when I kicked his darling son out for what he did in the labyrinth. Don't worry about that now. Let's see what comes to light. I could just be paranoid." She looked around the room to make sure no one had wandered into earshot.

"But don't be alone with either of them. Elios and Gavin are up to something. Maybe something bigger than guild membership. I'll object when Elios makes the announcement. I still have some say as your mother. Just remember you aren't alone, sweetie. Don't let them make you feel like you are. Make them fear you. Never cower. Never bend. Lie low and wait for the right moment to strike." Selene gave her a quick strong hug before she blended back into the crowd.

10

A bell rang three times. All conversation came to a halt. Every head in the room turned toward the stage. The king really did love the spotlight. Kane handed her a drink from a clockwork butler's tray as it passed.

"Up for a game of silvertongue?" Kane whispered in her ear.

"Always." Amber ignored the flutters in her chest caused by his breath on her ear.

"Welcome friends and family. Raise a glass." Elios began. "Tonight, we have much to celebrate. Our kingdom is the most peaceful and prosperous in its history. The peace is due in part to the work of our beloved witch hunter squad."

"Lie." Kane whispered. They both took a drink.

Elios continued. "To that end, I want to give a special acknowledgement to witch hunter Gavin Wade. He is a real all-star. Last night, he caught the *leader* of a witch rebellion that was planning an assassination attempt on myself and the royal family. It seems that history has a way of repeating itself." Elios paused long enough to let the gasps and murmurs subside.

"Lie." Amber nudged Kane.

"When offered any prize in the kingdom for his service to the crown, Gavin rejected wealth, awards, and honors. He only asked to see the would-be assassin properly punished for her crimes. His humility touched my soul."

"Lie," Kane said.

"My love for my niece coupled with his dedication persuaded me to gift him my niece's hand in marriage."

"Lie." Amber drained her glass. *How many lies was he going to tell?*

Her uncle had never shown her any sort of love or affection. Only trials and tests. When she was a preteen, Elios dedicated part of his days to her court training. Even back then, he hated her and made sure she knew it. When she turned thirteen, he took her to the seers, to get a measure of her fate. It was an excuse to test if she could summon a familiar spirit. Her mother tolerated the lessons up to a point. She made sure Amber kept her powers concealed. Amber realized too late that her time with the king would've ended sooner had her mother known about the nightmares that followed the lessons.

Like all witchfolk, Amber could mentally tap into the aura energy of any object and control it using telepathy. She could make flowers grow and conjure fire without a spell. She didn't need a wand to transform water or move the clouds. Controlling people and animals was possible but deadly dangerous. It hurt like hell and exhausted her to use her powers without aid. Directing her energy through wands or her grandmother's bloodstone ring kept her headaches and muscle aches bearable. Bloodstones were natural focus gems able to tap into aura. They powered the guild's wands and sigils and were activated by spells. If a spell was improperly cast, the bloodstones didn't activate. There were no malfunctions. That's why healers used bloodstone in their mender tattoos. It was like having a wand on your wrist. A very useful tool for emergency situations.

"In light of his work finding the assassin, I granted his request. You all will be able to see the would-be assassin in the labyrinth tonight." Elios smiled widely. "Gavin and Amber, please join me on stage so we can all celebrate your union."

He put Rynn in the labyrinth. Amber's head swirled. Her familiar screamed inside her chest. Her heart beat faster than normal. Heat flushed her face. Spells swirled on her tongue threatening to spill out in an angry flash. Instead, she redirected her rage through her bloodstone ring and directly at the king. Casting out a spell this far was hard but worth it. Amber pictured the words to summon the spirit of her familiar. *Invito virago.* The shadow of her griffin manifested on the king's shoulder. She dug a claw into his flesh. Elios' smile fell, his mouth twisting down at the corners. His face flushed. *Got you bastard.*

It was a copycat of the experiments he'd used on her when she was a child. A so-called 'guiding hand' powered by charmtek. He said it was a way to test her self-control under pressure. A skill needed for every royal, especially those not meant to wear the crown. She found out later he was trying to make her familiar manifest. If it weren't for the hidden cloaking charm on her wrist, he would've succeeded.

He used the spell on their strolls through the stonegarden while she recited the entirety of Kingslaw backwards and forwards. She still had nightmares of his orange glowing hand squeezing her shoulder until it bruised. Her royal lessons ended after her mother caught him in the act and raised holy hell. Her mom almost killed him that day, but she's settled for just taking off the tip of his ear. She called it a gift. Elios never struck back. That was the day she learned her uncle was a coward. He ran from confrontation because he was weak.

The crowd erupted in applause. Gavin snaked his way towards the stage, shaking hands, and bearing pats on the back as he shuffled through the lodge. Amber didn't move a muscle. Her mother was on the stage at Elios' side before he had a chance to react. Amber tightened her mental grip on the king. Despite using the ring, pain bloomed in her neck and temples from the effort. A cold pain bloomed in her wrist under her cloaking charm. Elios scanned the crowd, his eyes finally settling on hers. He tried to take a step away from her and faltered. She twisted the claw deeper. Elios touched a shaky hand to his clockwork necklace. She narrowed her eyes, twisting her claws into him further. Elios twitched, his hand dropping to his side. Sweat beaded on his forehead plastering his blonde locks to his face. The war was on.

"I'm sorry but the marriage you have planned will not be happening, dear brother. As you well know, Amber is a crownless royal. She isn't bound by your marriage promises and bargains. You can decide for your own children but not mine. Not her. Not ever."

"Kingslaw dictates that any marr—"

"Yes." Selene held up a hand. "Kingslaw. You respect that above all else, correct?"

"It is the king's duty to do so." Elios dotted his brow with a handkerchief. His cheeks grew redder by the minute.

"Then I ask that you respect Amber's marriage as it was entered into under that very law."

"You mean to tell me, Amber is married?"

"When you made your announcement, it was a shock to me. If only you had come to me with this news first, then I could have informed you that the prize you sought to gift to the hunter boy was not available."

"When did this marriage take place?" Elios narrowed his eyes. His blue steel stare bored into Amber. "Why was I not consulted?"

"Today. As it was told to me, Kane and Amber were swept up in the majesty of today's events and acted on impulse. You know how it is when love strikes. I mean it isn't surprising; they grew up together. He's her sworn protector. Really, is there anything more romantic? Their story mirrors King Wesley and Queen Celeste. You said it best, history does seem to tend toward repetition, sweet brother. You were young once. You understand."

"I see." Elios unclenched his jaw. "And was the bride-price paid?"

"It was." Selene smiled. "But I think it is tacky to discuss such matters in mixed company. We can discuss that later. Don't you agree?"

"I do." He rubbed the handkerchief across the back of his neck. "Well, that settles that it seems. Let us waste no more time on the love affairs of my niece." He clapped his hands twice.

The band set their bows to strings, filling the room with a lively melody. The noise did little to quiet the tension in the room and the pounding in her head. Amber unclenched her fists, releasing her hold on him. Elios rolled his neck in a circle, shrugging his shoulders as if trying to get a knot out. His gaze on her never faltered. He readjusted his crown over his scarred ear. Fear and recognition reflected in his icy eyes. He knew she was stronger than him. *Good. Medusa, let it give him nightmares.*

11

She leaned against the seat cushions of the clockwork powered watertaxi. The position forced her to unclench her shoulders. Although they'd slipped out of the lodge a few minutes after the confrontation with Elios, it wasn't a moment too soon. Her temples throbbed from the effort of binding Elios at a distance. Since her royal duties were over until the midnight dessert at the arena, they set their sights on finding the cipher. That meant going to the guild library. It was the only library in the kingdom with a collection of every volume of the Skyfarmer's Almanac. Not even the temples had past versions despite it being the kingdom's official holy book. The plan was to study the version in circulation during the last year of Queen Celeste's reign. It was their last hope of success.

Laughter cut into her thoughts. Kane and Zerrick sat at the front of the watertaxi, swapping stories and punching each other in the arms like old friends. Kane looked back and flashed her a smile. She hadn't had time to process the fact she was married now. She wasn't just staring at Kane, her best friend, and protecter. He was her husband. Everything was happening at light speed. They had hours to find the cipher, remake the witchblade, free Rynn, and dethrone Elios. It all felt impossible. But so had everything else that happened in the past few hours.

"Your mom humbled the fawk outta Elios," Jasmine said.

"She handled it better than I would've," Amber said. "He deserved worse. He put Rynn in the labyrinth. She isn't a fighter. Fawk! I'll kill him for this."

"I have to believe she's going to be okay. You do too. Don't lose hope yet. The king will get what he deserves. We just have to translate the spellbook first."

"Do you really think the Almanac is the key?" Amber glanced at Zerrick. "I mean, if that's it, how has no one figured it out yet?"

"Because the histories erased key facts about Vera and the queen. Think about how many new charms and spells we found in the spellbook so far. The spy rings. The portal charms. Queen Celeste was doing craftwork the guildmasters still consider theoretical. I would kill for a chance to learn from her."

"Big same."

"What I can't figure out is if she was so powerful, why would she use a poisoned pear to kill King Wesley? There are cleaner, safer ways to do it."

"I doubt she did really try to kill him. It was probably a lie so he could steal her work to take the credit," Amber said. "Kingslaw states that Wesley invented the quicksilver cure for witchfolk. But what else did he do? His focus was on turning the kingdom against witchfolk. He didn't do anything else significant. If he was the one that made quicksilver, he would have kept inventing after the queen was stoned."

"Quicksilver *cure*. What a joke. The histories have it all backwards. It's a curse. I hate that her spellbook is the only text that calls it what it is."

"There may have been more before Elios burned the libraries." Amber stared at the starry sky as they glided down the canal. "Wild how easily it was all lost."

"Hell, we don't even know what was lost."

"Or hidden." Amber pulled the puzzlebox from her satchel. "If Kane's great-grandfather hadn't kept this and the spellbook hidden away for the queen, we wouldn't even know there was a cure."

The puzzlebox was the biggest mystery out of the pair. At least the spellbook was a recognizable object. But this was an object straight out of lore, a reverie. Capable of holding memory projections and sending secret messages. What secrets had the queen hidden inside?

"Hold on. We're entering the tunnels." Kane called over his shoulder.

Amber tightened her lap belt and grabbed onto the safety bar to her right for support. The only thing she hated more than heights was descending the underground waterfall. During her first year at the Guild Academy, she'd spent a week at a time holed up in the library dorms so she wouldn't have to make the journey daily. Most of her classmates thought it was cowardice on her part, but it was something more. Each trip was a gamble with her life. The tunnels were a security system, blocking unregistered witchfolk from accessing the library. If the enchantment cloaking her witch blood from detection ever faltered while she was in the tunnels she would've been drowned or turned over to the witch hunters.

She held her breath as they passed between the two clockwork dragon guardians flanking the tunnel entrance. Their copper gears spun and glowed orange as their boat passed between them. The descent lasted an agonizing two minutes of near free fall. Amber practiced her breathing while counting the lights dotting the tunnel walls. Once they cleared the waterfall, it was smooth sailing down the winding river.

"You two should visit the Inkmasters while we're here," Jasmine said. She unwrapped a cookie-filled napkin she'd brought from the lodge. She passed a blueberry and honey one to Amber.

"You think splitting up is a good idea? We could go get the book then go to the Inkmasters together."

"We'll draw more attention in a group than as two couples. If anyone asks why we aren't at the arena, Zerrick is taking my confession and you two are smitten over your wedding and want to be alone."

"You sure you aren't just trying to get some alone time with a certain strong silent type that's unmoved by your powers?" Amber wiggled her eyebrows. "What are we settling on, Zerrmine? Jerrick? Just say the wor—"

"Eww. Shut up. Don't be gross. This is serious. We're running out of time." Jasmine bumped her with her shoulder. "Besides it would be Zasmine if we're doing that."

"I knew you were into him." Amber made a kissing face.

The watertaxi stopped before Jasmine could respond.

The guild library loomed before them like a castle from a fairytale. It was seven stories tall with four gleaming towers rising out of the corners. Each tower rose another thirteen stories high, nearly scraping the cavern's ceiling. The entire building was constructed of black glass and white marble tinged with ribbons of emerald and ruby. A nod to the coloring of bloodstone. A series of black glass skybridges connected the towers in a crisscrossing maze. It was clearly the work of earth mages. Amber sighed. It was criminal that something so beautiful was home to the black-market that sold bits and pieces of the very people responsible for its creation.

As they entered the library's atrium, they passed through another pair of clockwork dragon guardians. Flatscreens hung on every wall in the main entryway, a recent addition since she graduated. Each showed different parts of the arena. The foxhunt was underway. Jasmine and Kane checked in at the front desk while Amber watched the replay of the opening of the match. A copper and silver clockwork fox sat a few feet from the entrance of the labyrinth. A bell rang and it took off running towards the exit. The first set of fourteen air mages entered the labyrinth in a spread out in a line, wands raised, heads on a swivel. The image on the screen jumped and displayed a split screen. On the left, the rankings list showed a zero next to one of the names. The right side of the screen showed the scorched body of a grey-haired man. Goddess, the dragons worked fast. *Medusa, please keep Rynn safe.* She'd be the last obstacle for the mages. With any luck they'd be killed by the other folk before it was Rynn's turn.

"We'll go pull the Almanac and start looking for the cipher. Meet us in the reading room when you finish," Jasmine said. "Be careful and don't do anything stupid."

"You know me."

"Seriously, we have to leave in an hour if we're going to make it to the arena on time."

"I promise on my royal honor." Amber winked at her.

12

The confrontation with the king left her doubting their plan. There was no way to confirm if the questioners had broken Rynn or if it was all a bluff. Either way, the king had already planted seeds in the mind of the nobles to bring himself sympathy. Amber didn't have the elites' love on her side. The odds were good that their plan would be seen as a coup before it was seen as a resistance movement. The king was a problem. The black-market held the solution.

The elevator climbed the tower slowly towards their seventh-floor destination. Amber rubbed her thumb over the inside of her wrist. The motion did nothing to stop the cold ache of the angry magic. Her cloaking charm had worked overtime in her battle with the king.

"So, what's the real plan?" Kane asked. He leaned against the back wall of the elevator.

"What? Why do you say that?"

"Because I know you." He nodded at her wrist. "You hurt yourself at the lodge, didn't you?"

"No. I'm fine. It took more effort than I expected. I don't know if I'm out of practice or if it was the distance. But something was off."

"You've been stressed all day, maybe that was it." He wrapped his hand around her wrist and cast a healing spell. "*Invito curation.*" As he gently eased her pain, the mendermark on his wrist glowed a soft green.

Relief flooded her body. "Thank you."

"So, are you going to make me ask about your plan again?"

"I need a hunter's binding lasso."

"Of course you do. Which means going to the black-market. And you're using it for..."

"In case shit goes sideways."

"When does it not?" Kane shook his head. "Maybe I shouldn't have pushed so hard to come here. I know how it affects you."

"Listen. I'm in control. I'm on my best behavior. No experimenting. No fighting. No gambling. I'm sticking to the plan. Cross my royal heart."

"Uh huh sure. Heard that before, princess."

The elevator doors opened directly into the studio lobby. A glass check-in counter sat in the middle of the space, directly across from the elevator bay. Five workstations lined the right wall. Each had a recliner, stool, and worktable with attached mirror. The wall on the opposite side was lined with large flatscreens that showed different angles of the foxhunt. The couches in the lobby were empty. One lone inkmaster was working. He sat in a chair at the counter with his back to them, fully engrossed in the flatscreens. His hair hung down to his shoulder blades in single midnight black braid. It stood out in stark contrast to his yellow suit.

"Hi. Happy Foxhunt Day. I'm Kyron. What're ya looking to get today?" The man asked without turning in their direction.

"Just a couple guild sigils. Water and fire," Kane answered.

"Leave your licenses on the counter and grab a seat. I'll be with you in a minute. They just released the dragons. I want to see this." He waved a hand at the seats to the left side of the counter.

Kane followed the directions then joined Amber on the couch. Amber scanned the flatscreens for the rankings and death count. Eight contestants were left. Five more dead in the short time since they entered the building. Two tiger-sized blue and purple dragons galloped through the labyrinth, their coats a vibrant shock of color against the black granite walls. The screens captured the attack from different angles. The aerial view showed the blue dragon chasing five of the remaining mages towards the center. A second angle was the purple dragon's point of view from the next bend in the pathway where he lay in wait. The fight was an ambush. Once surrounded, the dragons unleashed two streams of black flames on their hunters. Smoke engulfed the air mages. When it cleared, only a medium-size pile of white ash remained.

Amber cheered inwardly. Whoever the dragon witchfolk were, they had survived for now. If they lived until the end of the foxhunt, they'd be set free. Of all the punishments for the folk, the labyrinth challenge was the cruelest because it gave them hope of freedom. Yet very few of them survived two days of mage battles to escape their captivity. Many could beat the air mages. Some survived the water guild's tricks. But almost none could defeat fire guild. Whether by trick or luck, her guild was the most successful when it came to the foxhunt; more than half of the champions were fire guild.

"Hell, yeah! The mages don't stand a chance." Kyron spun around on his stool. He picked up their licenses from the counter without looking up. "So, who's getting the water mark? Kane Vaughn or Amb—" Kyron's head snapped up, his eyes wide.

Amber raised her hand, flashing him a glimpse of her royal mark. It shimmered against the golden skin of her wrist as if lit from the inside.

"Oh shit! Princess. I'm sorry to make you wait. If I had known, I would—"

"It's just Amber and don't worry. We're not in a hurry," she lied.

"Wait. If you're getting a water mark. And he's getting a fire mark..." Kyron turned his head between them in a double take. "Then that means...Oh. Ohh. So the king's announcement was...wrong? You aren't betrothed to the hunter huh?"

"Nope." Amber smiled.

"How interesting." Kyron held took her by the hand and led her to the recliner at the center station. "Let's get you right, just Amber. You're only a newlywed once."

Amber lounged in the recliner. One flatscreen showed the surviving air mages moving together in a huddle towards the middle of the labyrinth. Another displayed the prize awaiting them at the center, a copper dagger embellished with pear-shaped emeralds. The blade was meant to be used to symbolically kill the fox if it was caught. A shadow flickered at the side of the screen. Amber squinted. The shadow shimmered before it settled back against the wall. The pair of unicorn witches. They were larger than the dragons, but not as strong. Their advantage was their mirage illusion. It allowed them to camouflage and attack by surprise. But the mirage was slipping. How long had they been hiding there? *Medusa, guard the mirage. Let it hold long enough for them to beat the air mages.* The witchfolk didn't deserve to die like this.

Kane stepped to her side then placed a hand on her shoulder.

"Aren't you two the cutest. The princess and her protector. Oh, my goddess! I just realized! You're just like the queen and king Wesley. Hopefully less tragic of course but didn't they start out so sweet." He handed her a small book. It was open to a page with images of four beautiful unicorns, each a different shade of blue. "The official guild sigils. If I may make a suggestion? Number two is the twin to Kane's."

"These are beautiful," Amber said. She ran a finger over the one Kyron suggested. "I'll take it. Thank you."

"Good choice. Alright then, let's get started." Kyron pushed up the sleeves of his jumpsuit. He took the book back and rolled a stool over next to her. "This may tickle a little."

Using the mirror Amber watched him. He picked up a penknife with two buttons that glowed orange. Fear gripped her chest. When she sat for her first sigil, the inkmaster used her wand. This penknife was charmtek. Amber sat up.

"Your penknife. It's so unique. When did you all start using those?" She tried to keep the nervousness out of her voice.

"This? It's a charmpen. Custom made charmtek. Just got it last month. I'm trying to convert the others to use them, but you know how hard it is to change tradition. Then again maybe you don't, little miss runaway bride."

Amber laughed. "And it's safe?"

"The safest. My friend makes them. She makes all types of gadgets. Nothing I've ever bought from her has had any charmtek glitches. She is the best."

Amber didn't have any other options. He was the only inkmaster working and she needed the guild sigil to access the water guild.

"Okay. Let's give it a try."

Kane held her hand as Kyron began his work. Amber kept her eyes focused on the mirror. Kyron picked up the charmpen from his workbench. He dipped the tip to the image in book then pressed a button on the side. An orange shimmer pierced the air along with a small buzzing sound. A cool sensation flooded her body when Kyron delicately touched the penknife to her neck. *Thanks, Kane.* The image of the unicorn bled onto her skin in an instant.

"Okay. All set."

"Thank you. You do wonderful work." Amber turned her head left-to-right so she could see how the two marks looked together.

Kane climbed into the recliner. He chose a fire guild sigil that was the twin of hers. Kyron repeated his task with the charmpen to place the black and red dragon on Kane's neck.

"You said they were custom made, what made you switch from using your wand?"

"They are much easier to use for removing guild sigils. When we have to strip the rejects, it can be a brutal process. This is a little easier."

Her thoughts drifted to her cousin. The spare prince probably couldn't handle the pain, he was a coward like the king.

"Hypothetically, where could someone go to get one of those charmpens?"

"Go see Navessa. She has a little gadget shop on the sixth floor. The Charmcatcher."

"The black-market," Kane said. "Of course it's dark magic."

"Down here, we just call it the market. Whatever you do with what you find there is a reflection of your heart, not the magic sold. Even dark magic can be used for light."

"I couldn't agree more." Amber smiled. Her backup plan was shaping up nicely.

13

Her shopping list was short. Kyron had assured her Navessa had everything. *Medusa, let him be right.* She'd only visited the black-market once before. In her last month at the academy, Imani had given her a puzzling task: unscramble an egg. She couldn't understand how it related to potions, but she was determined to solve it.

Amber had read every spell in the potions textbook but failed to find the answer. Even Jasmine couldn't find the answer after searching the spellbooks for the other subjects. They'd spent hours in the library. Jasmine did the reading while Amber crafted the spells. They used dozens of eggs in their experiments.

When she was ready to give up, Gavin offered to help. Amber was so desperate for the answer she'd accepted without asking any questions. That was her first mistake. Gavin said they had to go to the black-market. Her second was ignoring Kane's protests about taking the journey. They'd both heard the same rumors of cannibal foodies, but Amber brushed them off as mere urban legends without any merit. Their visit to the Bone Apothecary proved her wrong. When Gavin offered her a piece of dragon witch jerky she snapped and partially slipped into her familiar, bearing her fangs. Kane had to drag her out the shop before she attacked Gavin. It was a stupid mistake, but he had been asking for it; he claimed it wasn't *technically* cannibalism since the witchfolk weren't *technically* human. She shuddered at the memory.

Kane stopped in front of third shop from the elevators. "The Charmcatcher" glowed in green letters on a window sign. "This is the place."

He opened the door to let her enter first. The smell of cinnamon bread filled the shop. Amber felt a rumble in her stomach. It had been too long since she'd last eaten.

"Welcome to the Charmcatcher! I'm the owner, Navessa. What charm can I help you catch today?" The woman behind the counter greeted them with a smile. She was dressed in a tight yellow bodysuit paired with an oversized green sweater. Her eyes were the color and shape of almonds with flecks of green that matched her outfit.

"Hi. Your shop is lovely. It smells great in here. Kyron said you might be able to help us. I have a small list," Amber said. "I need two copycat books, a black bamboo wand, a charmpen, and a binding lasso, please."

"Oh, we have books on aisle forty. And the witch hunter's lasso is in the very back with the other weapons. Wands are on aisle twelve. It will be much easier if we let my charmcatchers get everything for you." Navessa snapped her fingers. A clockwork basket rose from a pile and floated over to her side. The gears glowed a soft orange as they spun against its copper framework.

"Oh!" Amber took a step back.

"Sorry. My charmcatcher baskets always *catch* people off guard." She laughed at her own joke. "Haven't had much business today because of the foxhunt. You picked a good time to run your errands. Come sit down while the shopping gets done. Can I get you a drink or snack from the bar while you wait?"

"Tea and that great smelling bread would be perfect. Thank you," Kane said.

"You're in luck. Fresh from Sinclaire's Sweets. It's the best sourdough in the market."

"Perfect. I love them. Thank you," Amber said.

Navessa led them to a sitting area near the store's display window. One of the clockworks brought a tray load with goodies. The bread was tangy and had a perfect crust. The lemon ginger tea was warm and the perfect match to the bread.

She was thankful for the flatscreen in the sitting area. The replay caught her up on what they'd missed. One of the unicorns was dead. Amber's heart ached at the loss. Unicorn witches were gentle and nearly defenseless against mages. There were only three air mages left. They were in the gargoyles' section of the labyrinth. Black marble statues the size of gorillas dotted the shadows of the twisting corridors. It was impossible to tell which were the true gargoyles. At any moment they could drop their camouflage and attack. The anticipation of it quickened her pulse.

The air mages walked slowly through the winding paths as they passed the statues. Shaky wands pointed at gargoyles in warning as the mages passed. They took a turn to the left and ended up on the path that was a straight shot to the exit. Two pairs of stone gargoyles lined the path to the final battle area. As they passed the first pair, the sound of glass breaking stopped the mages dead in their tracks. The gargoyle on the left groaned to life, shaking off the camouflage.

One of the air mages ran at full speed toward the exit. The other two were not as fast. The shorter mage held up their wand with a shaky hand. The taller and more muscular mage stepped back into the shadows. Standing on their hind legs, the gargoyle was a head taller than the mage. In a quick motion, the gargoyle reached out and grabbed the mage by the neck. The twist was quick and hard. The mage fell to the ground with a heavy thud. The gargoyle turned its attention to the mage in hiding. The mage screamed in panic. Slowly, a talon-tipped leathery wing stretched out and reached into the shadows. The mage's screams stopped.

Amber clinched her jaw. It was time for Rynn's battle.

She couldn't watch her friend get injured or worse. Her attention shifted away from the screen to Kane and Navessa. They laid out items from her shopping list on the table.

"Are you good?" Kane asked as he placed the items in his satchel.

"Yeah. Fine." Amber nodded.

"Charmtek tablet." Kane held up the device. "It links to the feed from the arena. Figured it would help us stay up to date on the foxhunt."

"Good thinking. Thanks," Amber said. Maybe charmtek was good for something after all.

"I made it myself. I'm a bit of a tinkerer." Navessa smiled. Pride coated her words.

"What made you want to use charmtek? It's so volatile."

"It can be but only if used improperly. The charmtek gems are quartz. They can hold charms, and they don't require spells. Enchantments can be placed directly on them for a specific purpose. The danger comes in if the enchantment is weak. The strength of the enchanter is much more important than with bloodstones. A wand is for multiple purposes. The charmtek gems only have the specific power given to them. Does that make sense?"

"It does." Amber nodded. "I feel better knowing it isn't powered by dark magic. But they are still glitchy. There've been accidents in the mines."

"I've heard about the accidents, but I think that is a harvesting issue more than an enchantment problem. You can put curses on the charmtek gems. But I can't imagine anyone doing that. There's too much chance the spell could misfire. I've never had any glitches."

"I trust you. Kyron used a charmtek pen for my sigil and it was painless. Big improvement over the wands."

"Thank you, princess. Do you need anything else?"

"It's just Amber. I have a weird question," Amber said. "Do you have anything that can unscramble an egg?"

"You mean a clocker spell?"

"I don't know, honestly. Is that like a mender thing?"

"No. it's something much different than the work of the healers. Why do you ask?"

"My potions teacher gave me the puzzle to solve my first year. But I never figured it out and she never gave me the answer."

"Probably because it's based on a folktale, Blackbird Princess."

Amber exchanged a look with Kane. He shrugged.

"It's an unofficial story. One that isn't in the Almanac. Probably because it has witchcraft. Funny thing is the story always reminded me of the queen's assassination attempt on King Wesley." Navessa ticked items off her fingers as she continued. "A jealous king. An evil huntsman. A poison pear. A witch princess cursed to sleep. And a magic crown to wake her."

"Sounds familiar. What was the charm they used to wake her?" Amber asked.

"A sunstone. The witch cursed her using a moonstone. The charm was the jewel's twin. It's a basic story about the nature of magic. Every curse can be charmed, and every charm can be cursed. If you know where to look."

"So, it was a trick question."

"I'm afraid so. If the egg was scrambled by a curse, you find the twin charm and you're in business. If it was scrambled any other way, there's no reversing it unless you invent a clocker spell to control time."

"Is there a way to locate the twin charm for curses?" Kane asked.

"A witch hunter's amulet can be enchanted to find lost living things. I don't know if it will work for anything else but it's worth a shot." Navessa snapped her fingers. One of the floating baskets appeared again. "Four hunter bloodstones, please."

The basket floated away. Within a minute it returned with its prey: a silver compass and a set of four black stones ribboned with emerald and ruby.

"I'd suggest trying them in different ways. The compass, an amulet, or whatever you think up. Just be careful."

"I will. Thank you." Amber gave her thirty gold coins for the items.

"Don't forget this." Navessa handed her a charmtek pen. It was identical to Kyron's.

"Thank you."

Kyron had more than delivered on his promise. She'd found everything she needed and more with Navessa. Now she had a better idea why King Wesley had banned witchfolk from the libraries. His lie about the queen was stolen from one of their folktales. Her mind wandered to the lessons Imani had given her. Was she missing something else that could help her remake the witchblade?

14

As she exited the shop, someone shoulder checked her hard. Amber looked up to see a witch hunter staring her down like she was his prey. He had the same shit haircut and musty scent as Gavin. Jack Alder, a bonehead in every sense of the word. Next to him his sister Pippy sneered at her with bulging eyes. The siblings were likely up to no good, but she didn't have time to wonder why they were there. Her focus was on what he'd mumbled when he knocked into her.

"What did you say?" she asked.

"He said, move *witch*." Pippy answered.

"Jackass and Pipsqueak. It's a displeasure to see you." Amber flashed a smirk at them. "Shouldn't you two be off somewhere kissing Gavin's feet?"

"It's *Jack*, witch. The only pipsqueak here is you." He pointed a dirty finger at her.

"That's enough. We get it. Your boss is mad, but you don't need to get hurt because of that." Kane took a step towards Jack, his arm slightly shielded Amber. "Do the smart thing. Move before I move you."

"Hiding behind your guard. Royals are such a joke."

"I got your joke right here." Amber flipped him off.

"Gavin's lucky he isn't stuck marrying your pampered ass," Pipsqueak said.

"Oh, you have no idea." Amber smirked. "Let's end this. Your dagger against my wand in the pits, *jackass*. First blood takes all."

"You wouldn't know what to do with it," Jack said. "I'm not wasting m—"

"He'll do it," Pipsqueak said. "We have some time to kill, and I could use the laugh."

"Oh, they don't know." Kane and Amber exchanged a look.

"No, it doesn't seem they do."

"Now, *that's* funny." Kane folded his arms across his chest.

"What are you two assholes talking about? What don't we know?" Anger deepened Jack's scowl.

"I don't protect her from the people. I protect the people from her." Kane smiled widely.

"Bullshit. You're trying to scare him into forfeiting."

"Believe what you want." She waved towards the sparring rooms with a sweeping motion. "After you."

The white sand pits were officially designated for student battles. But with the right coin slipped into the right hand, anyone could step into the ring. At only twelve feet in diameter, the circular pits where build for close hand-to-hand combat. It rewarded only the fastest among them. If you couldn't draw your wand or dagger faster than your opponent, you were as good as out the fight before it began. Amber didn't have that problem. She was one of the fastest quickdraws at the academy. Kane was the only mage who'd ever beaten her in the ring. It was no surprise the academy rejects had no clue about her skills. Not many people were willing to tell the story of being beaten by a princess.

They stood on opposite sides of the ring. A bell rang. Amber drew her wand from her shoulder holster, casting a shield charm just as Jack flicked a witch hunter's cuff at her feet. It bounced off her shield, missing its mark by inches. She kept her gaze on him as she bent down to retrieve the cuff. The binding charm felt heavy in her hand. She tossed it to Kane with a grimace. No way she was going to give him a chance to use it again.

"More hiding I see." Jack side-stepped around the outer edge of the circle. She was forced to mirror his movements in response. He feinted forward a couple times as they skirted the circle, measuring each other's weaknesses.

"Fighting dirty I see. Typical bonehead behavior," Amber said.

She pretended to trip, kicking up a small dust cloud. He took the bait. With a greedy look, he lunged forward, tossing his dagger at her shoulder. But his movement was too late. She cast a spell, stopping the dagger midair. It hung between them, a threat unfulfilled. Amber flicked her wand. She struck him on the arm with a slicing blow that cut to the bone. *That's for Rynn.* Jack cried out as a palm-size cut opened on his forearm. He pressed a dirty hand to his wound. It did little to stop the flow. Blood dripped to the sand and pooled at his feet.

First blood was hers.

"Better luck next time, jackass." Amber plucked the dagger from the air. She sheathed it in one of the empty leg holsters with a smirk. "I promise to only use it for good."

Jack flipped her off with his free hand. He limped away, hand clasped to his weeping arm. Pipsqueak sneered at her before following Jack away from the pit.

Amber thanked the goddess for her good luck. A cuff and quicksilver dagger were just as good as the witch hunter's lasso. Maybe even better depending on how the king retaliated.

"Good job, princess." Kane handed her the cuff. "Are you good?" He scanned her, his eyes lingering over her body long enough for heat to rise to her face.

"I'm fine. Really."

"Still need that lasso?"

"I think these'll do. Let's go see if Jasmine found anything."

"We need to hurry." Kane showed her his tablet. "The fire mages are entering the labyrinth."

15

As they rode the elevator to meet Jasmine and Zerrick, Amber watched the fire mage battle on Kane's tablet. They'd missed the water mages' round because of her fight with Jack. *Stupid.* A knot formed in her stomach. Her jaw dropped when the stats scrolled the bottom of the screen. Only one air mage had survived. She used trickery to slip past the last witch pair. Because she didn't kill to exit, she only received half the points possible for the round. The point system was sickening. There was no motivation to go for anything less than a death kill if you wanted to win.

That had been Kane's downfall. He was too kind for the battles. Kane used cloaking charms to slip past all the familiars and gain the lead. The dagger was his as he cornered the clockwork fox. But as with everything else, Gavin played dirty. Gavin had killed four familiars on his way to the finish line, taking body parts as trophies as he slaughtered them. So, when he attacked another mage, Kane knew the blow was likely fatal. He turned back from the griffins to help his fellow guild member. There was no reward for his bravery. In the end, he finished in second place. Amber's hatred for the king had deepened that day. *Thankfully, mom found a rule to kick Gavin out the guild for what he did in the labyrinth.*

More stats rolled on the ticker tape. All the water mages were dead. Amber was glad they hadn't watched after all; there was only so much death she could stomach in a day. Their losses were staggering. When was the last time that had happened? Circe was not smiling down on the mages today.

The stats switched to the familiars. The clockwork fox was still on the run, hiding in the shadows of the labyrinth. Both pairs of dragons and griffins had survived. Only one of the gargoyles had survived. The unicorns were dead. *Medusa, give them the peace in death that life denied them.*

Fourteen fire mages moved through the labyrinth like royal guards running a raid. They moved in a tight circular formation, wands up, heads on a swivel. One mage walked in the center of the circle, calling out commands. This was not good. Amber's stomach turned sour watching them work their way through the labyrinth. She recognized their strategy. Kane's dad had developed battle tactics based on strategies in royal chess. Kane had taught her about it during their daily spars. This was a pawn sacrifice. It was a simple but deadly approach. It relied on practice and trust. One mage was designated chess king, the most powerful player. The others were the pawns whose only objective was to protect the king at all costs. Someone had trained them for this. Amber was starting to rethink how much luck actually played a part in fire guild's success. *Please let Rynn survive.*

The purple dragon appeared from the shadows behind the mages. Three pawns broke formation to run interference. The ranks closed in, protecting the king. The mages were incinerated in a wash of black fire before he could finish his spell. Three down.

When the mages entered the center of the labyrinth, one of the pawns grabbed the dagger and passed it inside the ring to the chess king. Blue flame billowed out from the shadows and engulfed the back half of the pawns. Six dropped dead in a pile of ash. To their credit the remaining pawns reformed the circle without hesitation.

The mages barely made it halfway down the final corridor when a black shadow fell on them from above. The gargoyle was more vicious than the dragons. A fierceness flashed in their eyes as it attacked the formation from above. It reached down, plucking two from the ranks with their massive claws. When the headless bodies fell to the ground, panic set in. The chess king called out a command and the final trio sprinted out of the gargoyle area at breakneck speed towards the exit.

A pair of horse-sized griffins guarded the exit. The griffin with a thick black mane and white feathers sat stone still in front of the exit. If he didn't blink every few seconds, Amber would've sworn he was a statue. The metal fox sat between the griffin's front paws, its tail twitching back and forth. The griffin with a golden coat and green feathers paced back and forth with a slight limp that favored her right side. Rynn.

Amber and Rynn had shifted into their familiars together before Rynn would agree to join the coven. Kane had argued against revealing her biggest secret. Amber knew it was reckless, but it was the best way to show she was telling the truth about being a witch. Rynn had admired Amber's purple feathers and silver coat before shifting into her own griffin form. They swapped stories and took a short flight to stretch their wings. It was the first time Amber had shown another witch her real identity. Rynn was a true friend. When Rynn swore allegiance to the coven she picked kittyhawk as her codename. And now she was hurt and fighting for her life because of Amber. She cracked her knuckles as she watched her friend struggle to walk.

The three remaining mages stood at the end of the corridor, just shy of stepping into the griffin's domain. The chess king whispered something to the pawns who nodded in response. They split ranks, one pawn sprinting to the left towards Rynn. The other headed straight to the male griffin. The chess king stood at the entrance, holding the dagger in front of him with a shaky hand. Rynn let loose a roar that burst the eardrums of the pawn running at her. They dropped to their knees while blood dripped out their ears in dark wet lines. At the same time, the other griffin swiped a huge paw at the other pawn. He hit his mark, and the pawn skidded to the side then slammed into the wall.

Rynn's pawn recovered and was running at her with a spell spilling off his lips. The other griffin didn't hesitate. It took flight then scooped up the last pawn in his massive jaws before the spell could fall off his wand. The chess king took a few tentative steps toward the unprotected clockwork fox. Before he could strike, Rynn sprinted towards him with a roar. The chess king swiveled his head from the fox to the exit. His choice made, the king dropped the dagger and slipped through the exit.

A bell rang three times.

The first day of competition was over.

Rynn had survived.

16

Jasmine and Zerrick were waiting at one of the reading tables in the fiction section of the library.

"Why are we in the fiction section?" Amber asked.

"The third edition of the Almanac for the year the queen was stoned was split into two parts. But the first part was missing from the history section in the main collection. Zerrick guessed correctly that it might be shelved over here. It took some time, but we found it," Jasmine said. "What took you so long?"

"Okay, so look. It's not our fault. The inkmaster made us wait while he watched the dragons battle the air mages. Then we went to pick up the supplies at this cute little shop. The owner makes the coolest charms. So, tell me why when we left the shop, we ran into a couple boneheads."

"Girl, you always have a story. Who was it?" Jasmine raised an eyebrow.

"Jackass and Pipsqueak."

"And why did that take so long?"

"We went to the pits." Amber pulled the quicksilver dagger halfway out the sheath. "Took this from him. Real quicksilver dagger."

"That was reckless. He could've cut you." Jasmine frowned. "I'm not surprised."

"He started it," Kane said. "Besides, I was there. I wouldn't have let anything bad happen."

"Whatever." Jasmine waved it off. "We found something."

"The key to the cipher?"

"Sort of. There is only one entry for Medusa." Jasmine held up the open book to her. "It focuses on her constellation, Medusa's Sword. There's an explanation of its meaning and position. But the section on the cipher is blank. I may be missing something. I'll need time to read it."

"We don't have much time. Rynn is injured. She won't survive the battles tomorrow. We have to do this tonight."

"No pressure. Okay. We'll need to make a copy of the Almanac. Did you get the copycat book?"

"I got two just in case." Amber fished the books out her satchel then handed them over.

"Good. Tell them the other thing while I do this." Jasmine took out her wand.

She placed the copycat book on top of the Almanac. "*Invito reddo duo.*" With a whisper, she cast the mirroring spell. A glimmering flash of blue light encircled the books. Jasmine took the copycat and flipped through the pages, verifying the charm worked.

"Other thing? That sounds bad," Kane said.

"Well, yes and no." Zerrick turned the page in the Almanac. "This page has the Circe constellation, but the inscription is different from the official record. We think this volume was missed when the libraries were burned. Or someone left it behind as a reminder of the truth. The queen left behind the puzzlebox and spellbook with Kane's family. She allegedly gave Vera the witchblade. Maybe she trusted another family with this secret."

"Always have a backup plan." Jasmine muttered.

"Circe's Wand. Witch, warrior, and mother of mages." Amber read aloud. She flipped the page back to Medusa's entry. "Medusa's Sword. The queen of monsters." Green letters appeared in the blank section under the cipher heading. Witch ink. "Zerrick, you didn't see this message? It's written with witch ink."

"No. Let me see."

She slid the book back to him.

"It's blank." Zerrick frowned at her. "Where do you see something?"

"Under the cipher heading. But why don't you see it? We both can read witch ink."

"It's a legacy spell. It conceals things from everyone but the kinfolk of the mage who casts the charm. We learned about them in charms class," Jasmine said. She repeated the ritual with the other copycat book.

Amber didn't miss the academy. However, she did wish she'd studied harder while she was there. For the exams, the teachers only cared about how well you could cast and control the flame. Amber didn't have to study books for that. Her mom had taught her how to control her natural earth powers years before she was old enough to start at the Guild Academy. The breathing exercises worked to calm her nerves and focus her mind. Once she mastered that, conjuring and controlling the flame was as easy as making a rose bloom or turning water to ice. During school, most of her time was spent in the pits and the cafeteria.

"Is there any spell you don't remember?" Amber shook her head.

"Nope. Gift and a curse. What's the message say?"

"The truth lies where sword turns wand."

"I think you found the cipher!" Jasmine said. "Now we have to figure out what these two entries have in common. Once we do then we can translate the spellbook."

Hope bloomed in Amber's chest. They'd done it. Well Jasmine and Zerrick had. She breathed a sigh of relief. This trip had been worth it. After weeks of sneaking into the royal library in the palace and coming up empty-handed, this was a miracle.

"How long will it take you to crack the cipher?

"Before the play is over."

"Perfect. Let's go. We don't need any attention for showing up late."

"You know this changes everything, right?" Kane said. "Circe is the goddess. If people find out the truth that she's a witch, that could turn the kingdom upside down."

"That's what I'm banking on."

17

They had two options to exit the library, skytrain or skylift. Neither option was ideal given her fear of heights, but Amber picked the skylift. It was faster and the private cars gave Jasmine a chance to work freely. Powered by charmtek gems, orange bolts of charm energy rippled through the cables hoisting them to the surface.

A knot formed in her stomach as her thoughts drifted to what would happen if the charmtek failed. There were glitches across the city, but the crown kept them quiet through coin and imprisonment. Every time the coven tried to verify what happened, the people were too afraid to talk. She kept her wand at the ready in case it failed. There had never been a glitch at the library, but she couldn't shake the fear.

"We're not going to fall," Kane said. His thumb traced small circles on the royal mark on her wrist. "Promise. How about we work on the plan. Yeah?"

"Yeah." A sense of calmness washed over her. He really was a marvelous healer. He knew when she needed him the most and always showed up. She leaned into the distraction. But she kept her wand up.

"Do you want to loop your mom in before or after you make the witchblade?"

"After. The king is going to be on high alert after what happened at the lodge. I don't want to give him any sign that we're up to something."

"Not to mention Gavin. I don't think it was coincidence the boneheads were at the library when we were. I don't trust them."

"Me either."

They spent the rest of the ride working out the details of how to pull off their plan. The skylift station exit deposited them onto the street across from the guild office. It was too dangerous to portal into the royal box now. They hopped in a four-seater hovercab with a clockwork driver. Zerrick sat next to Jasmine in the backwards facing seat as they journeyed across the city

"Done." Jasmine grinned. "We have the password for the puzzlebox, blackbird. And the spell for the witchblade is fairly simple." She passed Amber a piece of paper. "You'll need a few items, but it shouldn't give you any problems."

Amber read it. Moonstone. Sunstone. Quicksilver. *Greenblood.* She looked up with wide eyes. Was it that simple? They were the original house symbols of the guilds. Moonstone for fire. Sunstone for air. Quicksilver for water. Blood for the witch guild. She'd seen the symbols combined with their animal mascots in books and on the old crests hanging at the academy, but she had no idea of their importance.

"Greenblood? Really? The last time I heard that word, my dad was knocking the teeth to the back of the throat of the mundane that said it to him," Zerrick said.

"That's what it says. I don't think the queen meant it in a bad way." Jasmine placed a hand on his arm. "I think it's the legacy spell again. Queen Celeste was making sure only her witchfolk kin could use the spell."

"That's weird. The shopkeeper in the black-market told us about moonstone and sunstone in some folktale about a cursed princess."

"Blackbird Princess. My dad used to tell me that one at bedtime," Zerrick said. "I liked it because she could shift."

"That explains the title. Circe's favor is on us." Jasmine placed a hand over her heart. "Amazing."

"You're amazing," Zerrick said. "I don't know anyone who could decode anything that fast. The temple is full of scholars that would kill to work as fast as you."

"It was easy once Amber found the cipher. And if you hadn't found the right volume, I wouldn't have anything to work with." Jasmine shrugged.

"You put it all together so fast. Is it because your mom is a teacher?"

"Yeah. She loves language and books. She let me sit in on her lectures when I was little. I guess I'm a quick learner. But we've been working with hundreds of ciphers trying to decode the spellbook." Jasmine shrugged. "Once Amber wrote the cipher down, I could see the strange spacing in the letters of the hidden message. The spaces matched the shared stars in the Medusa and Circe constellations. I created a stencil by punching holes in a piece of paper. It isn't hard to make once you know where to start."

"How does that work?" He asked.

"Like a paper magnifying glass. You place it on top of the encoded text, in this case the spellbook, and you get a new message."

"Like I said, amazing."

"He's right. We couldn't have done this without you. Thank you," Amber said. "Our parents couldn't do it, and they had the spellbook for months before they asked us to help."

"What? Why did they keep it from you?" Zerrick asked.

"Family tradition." Amber chuckled. "My grandmother had it her whole life, but she never told my mom. Mom didn't find the spellbook until years after she was dead. At least she told me a few months after she found it. I think it was because my grandmother's murder shook her up."

"Murder?" Zerrick scrunched his brow. "I thought the widow queen's death was an accident."

"Accident is the official story. My mom told me the truth when I was thirteen right after I summoned my familiar the first time. She wanted me to understand how dangerous the king was. Basically, Elios was tired of waiting for their mom to die so he could take the throne. After my grandfather died, my grandmother took the throne as regent.

It was only supposed to be until Elios came of age. But by the time they were five years past that date, she thought he was unfit to rule. My grandmother told them her plans to step aside on their twenty-sixth birthday and name my mom as the heir. Elios snapped. He killed my grandmother as a birthday gift to my mom. He took the throne while she was mourning. The rest is history."

"Goddess. I had no idea the king was that vile," Zerrick said.

"He's dangerous and ruthless. He used to give me lessons in court etiquette as a kid." Amber shook her head. "Long walks through the stonegarden, pushing me to recite the Kingslaw backwards and forwards. He used charmtek to test me and catch me in a lie. My mom almost killed him when she found out. That's how he lost the tip of his ear. She's been waiting for his revenge ever since."

"That's why our moms started the coven," Jasmine said. "To dethrone Elios before he has a chance to strike back."

"And now we have the key to making the witchblade."

"So, what's the plan?" Zerrick asked. "Are we marching into the arena and confronting him in front of everyone?"

"If you want us all arrested, sure," Kane said. "We have to get the people on our side first. That means getting the guilds on our side. They will follow the guildmasters' directions. We have fire guild thanks to Amber's mom. We know Nevin is never going to bring the water guild to our side. It all rests on the air guild. The side they take will influence everything."

"My mom has slowly been working on my dad. He says he's on our side but the secret meetings with Elios have her worried," Jasmine said.

"First we need to make the witchblade and test it before we do anything."

"Then we set a trap for the king." Kane grinned.

"Exactly. At dinner, my mom told me to lie low and wait for the right moment to strike. We're going to sneak out of the play during intermission. I can make the witchblade in the stonegarden."

"What about Rynn?" Jasmine asked.

"We're going to break her out during the witching hour. The guards are superstitious. We're going to use it to our advantage."

"Sounds fun. But I can't be out during the witching hour." Zerrick tapped his left cuff.

"The stonegarden is still palace grounds even though it's abandoned. As long as you're with me or Amber, you're fine," Kane said. "It's a little-known exception for royals so palace activity isn't hindered by the witchmaids having to stop working."

Fireworks lit up the sky as they pulled onto the street in front of the arena. It was the fifteen minute warning before curtains up. She'd missed the procession. *Shit. Shit. Shit.*

18

They hustled into the arena with the last of the stragglers. The concourse was lined with dessert tables piled high with sugary treats from Sinclaire's Sweets. Jasmine made a beeline to the fritters. She handed Zerrick a paper bag to hold as she dropped them in. Amber filled a bag with apple donuts and orange cake. She was so caught up deciding on her next pick that she jumped when Jasmine grabbed her elbow. Amber looked up to see Jasmine staring across the concourse at Gavin. He leaned against the wall next to the drinks table with his arms folded across his chest. He stared at her, a storm brewing in his eyes.

"You two go. We'll be okay." Amber whispered. "Stick to the plan."

Jasmine nodded and led Zerrick away towards the air guild section. They each had their strengths, and fighting was not Jasmine's greatest skill. She wasn't helpless but if Amber had the chance to shield her best friend from battle, she would. Amber locked eyes with Gavin. She matched his energy, crossing her arms and returning his death stare.

"Silverby. Vaughn." He walked towards them with his right hand resting on his dagger hilt. "I see you two are enjoying your little stunt. The black-market is a pretty cheap honeymoon if you ask me. What happened? You finally decide to have a little taste of the wild side?"

"It's *princess* Silverby to you, bonehead." Amber's stomach flipped at the mention of the black-market delicacies. "And where I go and what I do is none of your damn business."

"Did you two think this through? Even a little bit? What gives you the right to defy the king? Maybe you're just stupid."

"You lost, *champ*. Plain and simple," Kane said. "Whatever your plan was. It's over."

"Oh, that might be true. But I have another plan now." He stepped with an arm's length of them.

"No. One. Cares. Bonehead. Get a life or at least stay out of mine," Amber said.

"I think you'll be interested in this plan." He took another step forward, dropping his voice to a whisper. His breath stunk of spiced rum. "I heard a rumor that there's a witch in the guilds. Apparently, some witch is pretending to be normal. Imagine that."

"And you called me stupid?" Amber chuckled. "You're a fool if you think a witch could get past the guild's security and protocols. You should remember how strict the guildmasters are from when you got kicked out. Or is your memory as shit as your haircut?"

"I remember that your mom pulled a dirty trick using an ancient rule to get rid of me." He drummed his fingers on the dagger's hilt. "You know what I think? Maybe this secret witch had help. Like, I dunno, from a friend or even a *parent*. But who knows." Gavin shrugged. "I guess I'll just have to get my boneheads to arrest them and anyone who helped them. That'll give me the answers. I'm sure the king will find me a much better prize when I do. Your little air friend is single, right?"

"When's your brother's funeral? I would love to send my condolences to your parents." Amber tilted her head to the side while she batted her eyelashes at him. "Hopefully they won't have to bury another son soon."

"You threatening me?" He pulled on the hilt of his dagger to reveal a sliver of the blade.

"No. Just a warning that can turn into a promise, bonehead." She whipped out her wand and pressed it hard against his shoulder. "Maybe you want a scar to match your little jackass friend."

"You can't attack me here." Gavin's eyes widened. "It's against the rules to use your wand outside the labyrinth."

"Now, you care about rules." Amber pushed the wand harder. "Funny."

"Walk away," Kane said. "Now."

Gavin closed his eyes as he took a step back from the tip of her wand. "You'll regret this, witch. *That's* a promise." He took a few steps backwards before walking out the arena.

"Guess he's not in the mood for the theater anymore." Amber sheathed her wand.

"They know."

"I know. Let's just go." Amber took a few breaths to settle herself. "We'll have to strike first."

Silence hung between them as they took the elevator up to the royal box. Kane's dad, Tarkan, stood watch outside the royal box. He gave them a nod with a single message.

"Kittyhawk is in the kennels."

Amber's blood boiled at the mention of the holding pen for the foxhunt battles. They took their seats as the theater turned as dark as her mood.

19

The orchestra's violins and drums played a sublime harmony. The lights rose to reveal a transformed arena. Above the labyrinth, a round stage floated. It was decorated like an oasis. Dark green vines draped off the sides like a waterfall. A soft orange glow under the vines created the effect of fog surrounding the floating island. Belle Isle. Lush green grass dotted with red roses and white daisies covered the stage. A glowing sun hung midair above the center of the stage. A gleaming copper clockwork puppet wearing a flowing white gown stood at the center of the stage. It had blonde hair that flowed down her back in a cascade of curls. Amber marveled at how much the hair resembled her mother's. She wished she could talk to her mom, but it was impossible. The guildmasters and royal family were still sitting on the side stage. One mistake and their plans would be ruined. She had to settle for sending her a message using the spy rings.

"Welcome to the history of the Michigan Kingdom. Tonight, we will witness two betrayals that sunk the kingdom into war." The narrator's velvety baritone voice flowed through the speakers. "We start with the founding of our beloved city by the goddess Circe and her betrayal by the witch Medusa. The second betrayal shows how King Wesley survived the murderous plotting of the witch queen Celeste. We end with the rise of King Elios, the Tinkerer.

"In the beginning, goddess Circe left her island home to come to our world. She traveled on the tail of a shooting star. Finally making her home in a meadow nestled between the Moon and Sun rivers. Her only company were the animals, the wind, the moon, and the sun."

The Circe puppet bent down and picked flowers. With deft movements, the golden hands of Circe braided the flowers into a crown. The red and white crown fit perfectly on her head. A cluster of small woodland animal clockworks rose from a trap door in the stage. They scampered for a bit until they settled, sitting reverently at the feet of Circe.

"In a month's time, she met four travelers who had tracked the star to the isle. Upon finding that she was a goddess, they built a temple to honor her."

Four puppets dressed in brown riding clothes approached the meadow on horseback. They picked flowers and moved stones on the left side of the stage. An alabaster building rose up in the middle of their circle. Circe joined them at the building.

"Circe breathed ether into her devotees giving them the gift to control the elements. They used the gifts to nurture and tend the land."

The devotees knelt in front of Circe. She touched each one on the shoulder, their clothes transformed into the guild's colors. To the puppet in red she gave fire, a flame appearing in the puppet's hand. Adorned in purple, the air guild puppet hovered a half step off the ground. A fist-sized ball of water hovered over the palm of the teal clad puppet. A pair of golden and silver stones swirled in a hypnotic pattern in front of the puppet in green.

"Soon the meadow grew into a village and then a town and then a city. Our beloved capital city, Detroit. The success of Circe's temple drew the attention of dark forces. The witch Medusa found the temple during a blood moon."

Small buildings popped up around the temple. A clockwork puppet dressed in a green smock and cape rose up in the middle of the village. Medusa's snake-like hair flowed green, wrapping around her head like a living halo. The sun shifted colors, glowing red like a ball of fire.

"The witch brought dark magic and war to Circe's temple. The temple beat Medusa and Circe banished her from the land. But Medusa had won a small victory. The devotee with the gift over earth fell victim to her witch curse, transforming into a lowly woodland animal."

Green clouds encircled the red moon. Lighting ripped across the top of the stage. The symphony played a discordant tune to match the battle on stage. Circe and Medusa crossed sword and wand. Circe hacked the wand in half. She marched Medusa to the edge of the stage at sword-point. Medusa spun around, spitting out a curse that struck the stone devotee with a bolt of green lightning. The devotee dropped to the ground, transforming into a fox. Medusa fell over the side.

"Circe blessed the beasts and allowed them to stay as her devotees. She gave them a second gift, the ability to walk as men and control the beast within, only transforming at their desire. Things were good for millennia. The city grew into a kingdom. There was peace in the land for a time. Then dark magic again spread in the land, as the witchfolk ignored Circe's gift to walk as men. The great betrayal tore the kingdom apart."

Circe hugged the cursed devotee, its appearance transforming back to a man. The scene progressed through ages as taller buildings sprouted and more puppets gathered. Groups of puppets dropped to the ground shifting into witchfolk. A cloud of green fog spread across the stage. The moon turned green to match.

"Intermission."

Applause thundered through the arena. They slipped out of the box and into the hideaway portal just as the lights came up for intermission. She refused to watch the distorted telling of her grandmother's murder and Elios' murderous reign. His peace was colored with the blood of the witchfolk. So much of the truth was twisted, she wondered how to get the kingdom to learn the truth. She took solace in the fact that the lies about her family ended tonight. Amber had watched the play with fresh eyes; now it was time to open the eyes of the rest of the kingdom.

20

The stonegarden sat in the shadows of the old palace on the northside of Belle Isle. The groundskeeper's cottage sat abandoned at the back of the plot. Vines grew up the walls and along roof of the squat stone building. Although it was unguarded, the cursed grounds were off limits to visitors. While playing in the tunnels of the palace, Amber, Jasmine, and Kane had found a secret entrance to the stonegarden. After some exploring and testing, the trio picked the spot as their playground. Amber liked the view of Canada from the cottage. She had sat in the window and dreamed of visiting one day with her dad. The cottage was their clubhouse where they practiced spells, played games, and ate wild strawberries. Amber shifted freely during those times, learning to control her familiar away from prying eyes. It was also the place where she had her first kiss. Now the cottage served as the coven's headquarters.

Tonight was no game. This spell had to work or her mother and Rynn would be exposed to the king's unchecked wrath. She didn't have time to worry about her own fate since Gavin confirmed the king knew she was witchfolk.

"Everyone stand back." Amber twisted the rings on the puzzlebox until they spelled out the password, "blackbird." Amber set the puzzlebox down on the table at the center of the room before stepping back next to Kane.

The cap of the puzzlebox twisted open. Green smoke poured out, engulfing the table like an early morning fog. It was a reverie. The memory swirled for few seconds before images started to form. It started with the queen watching the king use the quicksilver witchblade to stone a witch wearing a monk's robe. *Vera.* Then came the queen's memory of forging of the golden witchblade with a guard watching. He shared Kane's strong jaw and kind eyes. *It had to be his great-grandfather.* The memory shifted to an argument with the king. The king put a binding cuff on the queen. Another shift. The queen woke Vera with the witchblade. She gave Vera the witchblade with a warning to hide. She gave the puzzlebox to the guard. Once the memory fog disappeared back into the puzzlebox, the cap twisted shut.

"Yes!" Jasmine clapped and jumped up and down.

Amber threw her arms up in victory. Kane grabbed her around the waist, scooping her into a hug. His heart throbbed against her chest in rhythm with hers. They locked eyes as he set her down, blood flooding to her cheeks.

"This is exactly what we need! No one could deny the truth after seeing this," Zerrick said.

"We did it!" Jasmine ran around the table and hugged her. "That means I was right."

"I never had any doubt." Amber turned to the table. "Now for the real work."

They watched silently as she worked the spell for the witchblade. Amber placed the spell ingredients and supplies on the table. With a quick prick of her finger, she squeezed four droplets in a black marble bowl. She placed the moonstones and sunstones on top of her offering. Green fire jumped from the palm of her hand into the bowl. The fire hissed and danced, shifting from green to black. At the bottom of the bowl, the ingredients had melted in a swirling green liquid. She stirred the mixture clockwise four times with the tip of the quicksilver dagger while casting the spell. *Apto pestis gladius.* The dagger jerked from her hand. It stood on its tip in the center of the bowl. Slowly, the green mixture crept up the dagger's blade. When it reached the hilt, the liquid shimmered and shifted to a beautiful golden finish that moved like water. Quickgold.

This was not the time for more celebrating. They had to test the blade. *Medusa, please let this be right.* Amber walked at Zerrick with the witchblade raised. He took a step back reflexively.

"For your cuffs." She shook her head.

"Oh, right. Sure." Zerrick held his hands out between them.

Amber placed the witchblade to back of the swirling metal cuff on his left wrist. A golden light flashed where the blade touched. The ripples in the quicksilver froze. The cuff turned ashen gray then cracked along the line where she touched it. She repeated it with the second cuff and Zerrick held his hands up to catch the falling metal. He touched his newly freed wrists, tears welling in his eyes.

"Thank you."

"I'm sorry it took so long." Amber brushed a tear from her eye.

"Not to rush you but the witching hour is halfway over," Kane said. "We have to hurry to get to the kennel."

They walked out the door of the cottage to find Gavin at the end of the path with her cousin, the spare prince Nazim. Two pairs of binding cuffs hung off Gavin's belt. Nazim held a hunter's lasso in his hand at the ready.

Amber took a step back in shock before regaining her composure. She raised her wand directly at Gavin's chest.

"What are you doing here?" Amber demanded.

"My job. Tracking criminals." Gavin eyed Zerrick. "What time is it, Naz?"

"Looks like the witching hour to me," Nazim said. He craned his head up towards the hollow moon.

"Just you two then? Where's jackass?" She looked around for Jack and Pippy.

"He's at the doctor. You destroyed his arm, witch." Gavin turned his attention to Zerrick. "Shouldn't you be in Witchtown, boy?"

"He's on palace grounds. You don't get to question him." Kane stepped in front of Zerrick. "This is palace business."

"The boy soldier defending a criminal. I'm sure your father would be proud," Nazim said. "I think I have more say in palace business than you, *servant*."

"Worry about your own father's disappointment." Kane ticked off his failures on his fingers. "No crown. No wand. Just ordinary. Just what a king wishes for in a son."

"Fawk you." Nazim yelled. He let a length of the lasso slip free of the loop. A soft orange glow radiated from a ring on his hand.

Gavin placed a hand on Nazim's chest to keep him from lunging towards Amber's outstretched wand.

"Listen, I'll make you a deal. The monk can stay. No harm no foul. But the witch princess is mine."

"I'll never be yours."

"You sound just like her." Gavin laughed.

"What are you talking about?"

"That's what your mom told my dad when she broke their betrothal. Apple doesn't fall far, huh?"

"What is it with you boneheads picking fights that aren't yours to worry about? The hell do you care if my mom married your dad? Get a life."

"It. Matters. Witch." Gavin unhooked one set of cuffs. "Your mom has ruined my family. She kicked me out the guild because she hates my dad. That's why I care."

"You seem confused. You were kicked out for violating the rules. You monster. You nearly killed Bowen for a damn dagger."

"No. Your mom is hellbent on hurting and embarrassing my dad. It wasn't enough that she rejected him and ran off to marry that bum ass foreign dad of yours."

Mom never said it was Nevin who she rejected. That explains a lot.

"My dad is the Canadian ambassador; he was born a noble. He's from the westside. You don't know what you're talking about."

"I know you're just like your whore mom."

"That was a stupid thing to say, bonehead." Amber flicked her wrist. "So was bringing a dagger to a wand fight."

She split her focus and attacked them both. Her familiar surfaced. It sent out two tendrils of power towards the hunters. The charmtek gem cracked, cutting off the orange glow. The lasso took on a life of its own, wrapping around Nazim's core, pinning his arms to his sides. A heartbeat later, Gavin dropped to his knees. His arm yanked above his head and twisted unnaturally. He dropped the cuff.

"Mercy." Gavin begged. Tears flooded his eyes. "Please."

"Sorry, fresh out of that." Amber sliced his pinky off with the quicksilver dagger. She summoned the familiar spirit back to her, partially shifting. Her fangs grew, twisting her lip into a snarl. "All I have left is vengeance."

The stone curse worked so fast he didn't even bleed from the cut. The ashen grey of stone spread from the incision up his arm. Gavin's face distorted as he watched the curse creep toward his shoulder. Desperate hands clawed at the graying skin. He slumped to the side with the weight of the curse.

"Don't make that face, it could get stuck like that, bonehead." Amber warned. She growled at him, her fangs fully on display.

"You damn wit—" The curse crept up to his lips before the word slipped out. His face froze with his mouth hanging open, brow scrunched in fury.

"Oops. Too late. Guess he should've listened." Amber kicked him square in the chest. The granite was lighter than she'd imagined. Gavin fell backwards with a thud, splintering into chunks.

"My dad is going to kill you when he finds out what you are, witch." Nazim gasped. He tried to crawl away, but the slick stones prevented him from getting enough traction.

The king didn't know. Gavin lied. Amber smiled inwardly. There was still time to get the upper hand in the cold war that brewed between them.

"Damn boneheads. You have a bad habit of saying dumb shit." Amber flicked her wrist, the rope tightened around him. His scuttling stopped. "Can you handle this please, captain?"

"Whatever you need." Kane knelt on Nazim's chest. He took out his wand then pressed it to the prince's temple. "The less you move the better chance you have of still remembering your name when I'm done." Nazim's eyes widened but he stopped squirming. "*Progredior sopor.*" Kane cast the forget-me-not spell. Nazim fell into a deep sleep. The sleep would convert his memories into distorted dreams, making him forget what he knew about Amber. Kane had used the spell once before when a guard caught them vandalizing a jewelry store that sold charms made of witch bones.

"Time to send the king a message." Amber picked up Gavin's head and then tucked it under her arm.

"Remind me never to piss you two off," Zerrick said.

"I told you they were a bit much." Jasmine hooked her elbow through Zerrick's. "But you'll get used to it."

"Are we just going to leave the prince here?" Zerrick asked.

"We'll come back for him," Kane said. He dragged the prince to the bench. "For now, he stays here out the way."

"Change of plans. We need to make one stop before we go to the kennels," Amber said. The puzzlebox was a great start to re-educating the kingdom but she needed more proof. She wanted to show them the curse could be reversed. And she knew exactly the statue to awaken.

21

Black vines wrapped around the legs of the stone queen. The hollow moon of the witching hour shone a green haze over the stonegarden. Amber stared up at her serene face frozen in granite while Kane cleared the vines. The weight of the responsibility weighed on her chest making her breathing too shallow. Breaking a cuff was a far cry from waking a statue. What would they do if this failed? What would happen to Rynn and her mom? Kane placed his hand on her shoulder. The quick gesture calmed her instantly. She nodded a thank you. He took Gavin's stone head from her then stepped back to where Jasmine and Zerrick waited.

Amber raised the blade above her head. With a swift and strong motion, she aimed the golden witchblade at the stone queen's heart. The blade didn't pierce the stone. Amber closed her eyes and hung her head. The witchblade failed.

She failed. The fight was over. She let her mom and Rynn down. Would the puzzlebox be enough to change the people's minds if they couldn't free the witchfolk from stone coffins? Had she made things worse by trying? A cracking sound pierced her downward spiraling thoughts.

"Look!" Jasmine said.

She opened her eyes. A spot of golden light glowed where the witchblade hit the stone. The stone on the queen's chest cracked into large sheets. Glowed golden cracks rippled across the stone body like shattered glass. The stone fell away into a pile of rubble at her feet.

The newly freed queen yawned and stretched, shaking her blonde curls loose.

She looked around then took a stumbling step forward. Zerrick rushed to her side. To steady her, he held the queen under the arm.

Amber's heart leapt with joy. It worked. Hope was standing in front of her.

"Thank you, monk." Queen Celeste looked around the stonegarden blinking slowly. With her free hand she twitched a tan finger at Amber beckoning her closer. "Come here child."

Amber slowly walked to her.

"You look just like my baby girl Dawn," Celeste said. She placed a soft hand on Amber's cheek, searching her eyes.

"I'm Amber. Dawn was my grandmother."

The queen's face crumpled with understanding. Zerrick led her to a wooden bench. Her gaze swept the sky.

"The stars are different. Tell me child, how many years have I been gone?"

"It's been one hundred years since you were stoned by the king."

"And what of his majesty? How did he die?"

"King Wesley was killed during a foxhunt."

"Good. I only wish that he had died by my hand." Celeste rolled her head in circle, stretching her neck. "Who was the lucky bastard that did the deed?"

"The assassin was never found. Legend says it was a royal guard."

"Luka Vaughn. Good job old friend." The queen smiled. "What of my Dawn?"

"Murdered for the throne by her son, Elios, the current king."

"Your father?"

"Uncle."

"I see. And you were the one to forge the witchblade?"

"With the help of my friends, yes." Amber swept a hand at them, "I couldn't have done it alone."

"Clever bunch. What are your names?"

"This is Captain Kane Vaughn, royal guard." Amber pointed at them in turn. "Zerrick Reeve, monk of the Green Temple. Jasmine Overton, heir to the air guild. We are the Medusa coven."

"Circe was smiling on us indeed. I guess you know your families were very important to me. Thank you." Celeste bowed her head to them.

"Can I ask, why blackbird for the password?" Jasmine asked.

"It was Dawn's favorite bedtime story. I thought it would help her find the answers if she went looking."

"Was my grandmother witchfolk? She died before I was born, and my mom doesn't talk about her much."

"Yes. She was the most beautiful unicorn. When she was two, she lost the power after she caught the dragon fever. I'll never forgive Wesley for unleashing that pox on the witchfolk."

"Wait. The Almanac said the fever was because of tainted milk from Chicago," Jasmine said. "That's why King Wesley stopped trading with the mundanes."

"It was a lie. The fever was a result of Wesley's experiments."

"So did he use a curse or potion?" Jasmine asked.

"I never found out. I just know that Wesley was obsessed with the witchfolk. He wanted to harness the familiar power for himself to make a witchfolk army. When he failed, he lashed out. He created the quicksilver curse to control what wasn't his to take. Why?"

"Dragon fever came back seven years ago. The crown said it was because of the uncleanliness of Witchtown," Jasmine said. "But now I wonder if it was a copycat."

"You think someone created the fever?" Zerrick asked. "That would be beyond evil."

"Well, the king *is* evil," Amber said. "He fears being weak. It drives everything he does. He will do anything to keep control over the witchfolk."

"Like burn the libraries." Jasmine looked at Amber. "Maybe he found something about King Wesley's experiments in the stacks."

"Maybe." Amber took a breath. "When I was younger, he experimented on me. He said it was to make me a better royal, but I know he was trying to see if I was witchfolk. I think that's why he wanted me to marry Gavin. Who else could get that secret out of me better than a hunter?"

"He sounds like Wesley. Everything he did to the witchfolk was to harm me." Celeste sighed. "He wanted my power and when he couldn't take it, he went berserk. He hurt people I cared about. When he stoned Vera that was my final straw. I just was too late to make a real difference. By the time I finished, he had destroyed the earth guild and banned witchfolk from the libraries. In the end, I could only help Vera and hope that someone else finished what I started."

"We can fix what he broke. We're going to break the cuffs, awaken the stonegarden, and restart the Earth guild," Amber said.

"What of your king?"

"We're taking away his throne and bringing him the pain that he unleashed on the kingdom."

"I'd like to meet him. I have some questions about my Dawn I'd like to ask him." Celeste stood. She stared at Amber with a fierce smile.

"I was hoping you would."

"Do you have an extra wand? I'm still feeling weak."

"I do." Amber handed her the black bamboo wand from her satchel. "But first we need to rescue my friend. They're keeping her in the kennels at the arena. We'll portal into the tunnels, grab her, and go to a safe house."

"Lead the way, child."

Amber walked through the stonegarden in a daze. *They'd actually done it*. Her eyes scanned all the statues. All the lives that were waiting to restart. All the grief for what and who they'd lost during their imprisonment. Her head spun at the layers of harm the stonings caused.

22

Kane drew the portal charm on the cottage door. They walked through and were transported to a supply closet in the kennels. The stale stench of urine and blood made Amber gag. She spit on the cobblestone floor to clear the bile out her mouth. The faint sound of the orchestra played overhead. Kane checked his tablet; they were near the beginning of act two. Despite the danger they were walking into, Amber was thankful she didn't have to sit through that trash. They decided Jasmine and Zerrick would stay hidden. The queen would disguise herself as a witch hunter under Kane's command. Amber would be a new gargoyle entry to the battles.

Amber took out the charmpen she got from Navessa. *Medusa, let this work*. She pressed the tip to her wrist. The cloaking charm glowed green. A cold burning sensation bloomed in her wrist, traveling up to her elbow. She gritted her teeth through the pain as the charm rose out of her arm and into the charmpen.

"You okay?" Kane asked.

"Fine." She rolled her wrist in a circle. The dull ache that was always with her was gone. She hadn't been pain-free for years. "Better, actually."

She took a deep breath and exhaled slowly preparing to shift into her familiar. *Invito virago*. The silent words summoned her gargoyle to the surface. The familiar needling sensation flowed through her body from the top of her head down to her fingers and toes. In a rush she felt her familiar takeover. Her body expanded and her muscles throbbed from the effort. She let out a low groan as she fully shrugged into her familiar. She was the same height as Kane now. Amber flexed her leathery wings before tucking them back against her shoulder blades. Her shoulders popped with the effort. Her nailbeds ached from the growth of her claws. She trailed an open hand along the brick wall, scratching the irritation away. A feeling of calm washed over her. Thanks to the cloaking clothes spell she used when shifting, her clothes still fit in all the right places.

"I'm ready." Amber's voice was raspy like when she had a cold in her human form.

They slipped out the closet, Amber turned sideways to fit her wings through the door frame. Kane and Celeste led the way. She trailed behind. Zerrick's broken cuffs hung awkwardly around her wrists. The dull color was noticeable if the guards looked too hard, but the risk was worth it. She needed to be at her strongest if they had to fight their way out.

Kane led them down the hallway past an empty guard station. At the end of the hallway, they could turn left towards the arena entrance or right to the cages. The impulse to rush up to the arena and wreak havoc on the king rushed through her. She hadn't unleashed her familiar in days.

When they turned right, the cages lay ahead of them at the end of the hallway. There was a guard desk halfway down the path. Kane led them in silence.

"Captain." The guard saluted Kane. "How can I help you?"

"King wanted to replace the gargoyle." He nodded to Amber. "For tomorrow's foxhunt."

"We weren't supposed to get replacements until the morning."

"Plans changed. Keys?"

"Sorry, captain. I didn't know. They never give me updates. I can open them for you."

"No. This one is dangerous. Caught it plotting with the griffin beast to kill the king."

"Oh shit. These beasts need to learn their place." He handed the keys over. "They already were fed for the night. It'll have to wait until the next shift comes at dawn."

"Thanks." Kane took the keys with one hand. He raised his wand with the other, hitting the guard with a sleeping spell. He slumped onto the desk with a heavy thud.

They ran to the cages. Amber got there first. In front of her, massive cages numbered one through four lined the walls. Each was bound by quicksilver bars and labeled with the beast types.

"Rynn!" Amber peered into the fourth cage labeled griffin.

An orange glow radiated from the shadows. The griffins huddled together at the far corner of the cage. The smaller one limped out of the shadows; her eyes bright with pain.

"Rynn. It's me Amber. Step back." Amber waved Kane forward. "We're getting you out of here.

"Amber? How? Wha—"

Kane stepped forward. He fumbled with the keys. A cracking sound came from their left. Amber turned toward the noise. Celeste walked in front of the cages; her arm outstretched. Amber pulled Kane away from the door. A heartbeat later, the queen walked past them, dragging the witchblade across the bars. The bars dulled; the swirling metal froze in place. The bars split at the line drawn by the witchblade. Amber reached out and pulled the weakened bars apart, creating a huge hole. Rynn stepped through followed by the male griffin. Amber wrapped her arms around Rynn's soft neck. She felt her friend relax and lean into the hug.

"Thank you," she whispered.

While the queen cut their charmtek collars off, Kane checked them for injuries and healed those in need. They handed out cloaking clothes to the witchfolk as they shifted to their human forms. Amber walked to the other cages, pulling the broken bars apart. The witchfolk stepped out tentatively. Amber marveled at how beautiful they were close up. The unicorn's coat shimmered an iridescent purple and green in the light. The dragons were more multicolored than the flatscreens had shown. The other gargoyle had beautiful skin the color of redwood and long silver claws.

"So, obviously this is a rescue. We're taking you to a safe house. You have to stay hidden until we send word." Amber explained what was happening quietly. "You'll have everything you need."

The witchfolk nodded in agreement.

"Why are you helping us?" The unicorn witch eyed Kane. "Guards like you put me in here."

"We're the resistance movement. We have people throughout the city working in secret to help."

"It's true." Rynn stepped forward. She had shifted back to her human form. "I'm one of them. They really want to help. Amber, I need to tell you something."

They stepped out of earshot from the group. Kane and Celeste joined them near the third cage.

"Is this the queen?" Rynn asked with wide eyes.

"I am." Celeste smiled. "Ignore me, child. Tell your story."

"Y-yes, your majesty. When I got caught last night, I overheard the hunters talking about something odd."

"Gavin?" Kane asked.

"Yeah. Gavin and Jack. I didn't understand all the words. He said something about Ediston, clockwork butlers, and a city of wind. I thought it was some hunter talk but their voices made it seem important."

"I'm glad you told us. We'll figure it out. Don't worry. You've been through enough." Amber swallowed. "I'm sorry I pulled you into this."

"It was my choice. I'd do it again if it means getting everyone free."

Kane drew the portal charm on the door frame. When he opened the door, it led to the basement of the safe house, the private home of the Canadian ambassador. It was the safest building in the city. Warded by backfire charms, it reflected the ill intentions of intruders back to them. The smell of roasting carrots, potatoes, and peppers wafted through the door. A man stepped through the door wearing a white apron embroidered with a red heart. His curly black hair was cropped short on the sides. His brown eyes shone brightly against the golden skin that matched hers.

"Hi dad. Thank you for this." Amber smiled widely, her fangs pressing into her bottom lip.

"Hi kiddo." He gave her a big hug.

"This is Canadian ambassador Tevin Gilbert." Kane introduced.

"Seems like you folks caught me at the right time. My veggie stew is almost done. Hope you all have appetites." He greeted them with a wave. "Come on in make yourselves at home."

Amber's heart ached at the sight of him. She had so much to tell him. About Gavin, Kane, the queen. It was all too much. He'd skipped the foxhunt as a statement against the treatment of the witchfolk. She didn't even know if he knew about the king's attempt to betroth her to Gavin.

Rynn gave Amber a quick nod and stepped through the door. The other witchfolk followed without hesitation.

"Your mom told me she put Elios in his place. I almost marched down to the arena myself when I heard his announcement. But I saw the look on your mom's face while he was talking. I figured she could yell at him better than I could anyway."

Amber chuckled. Her dad was a calm man; she couldn't imagine him yelling at anyone.

"You did the right thing by staying here. This is the biggest help ever. It smells delicious."

"When I got your message this morning that Rynn was arrested and you were going to bring her here, I started prepping everything. Do you want some food? I made a ton."

"No, we need to get back before any guards come. Oh! Dad, this is Queen Celeste."

"So, you did it. Good job kiddo. I knew you could." He bowed to Celeste. "A pleasure to meet you, your majesty."

"Just Celeste. Nice to meet you too. You have a special kid here."

"Don't I know it. Be safe kiddo. Keep her safe, captain."

"Always," Kane said.

They left the cage room in a line. Kane led the way with the queen in between them. As Amber passed the guard station a muffled groan floated up to her. A chair slid across the floor. Amber spun around to see the guard looking up at her with glossy eyes. She didn't have time to think. Instinct kicked in. A streak of black fire burst from her hands. It hit the guard square in the chest. Flame and smoke wrapped around him like a cloak. When they cleared, all that was left was a pile of ash. *Shit.* Killing the guard wasn't the plan. But when she sensed danger, her instincts took over. Her impulses were out of check. Maybe she shouldn't have removed the sigil.

"Guess you put him in his place." Celeste nodded at her with approval.

Amber didn't know what to say so she settled for a nod.

"Let's go before someone shows up." Kane hurried them to the closet.

Outside the door, Amber shifted back to her human form. When the door opened, Jasmine and Zerrick were sitting on the floor, their heads inches apart, bowed over Kane's tablet. They startled as the trio walked into the closet.

"S-so? Are they at the safe house?" Jasmine asked. "Did it work?"

"Was there any doubt?" Amber smiled. "How's the play going?"

"They are starting act three." Zerrick answered. "They're at the part where the king takes the throne."

"Okay, so we have a little over an hour until it's over. Just enough time to build the arsenal and gather the coven. Then we go see the king."

23

In the basement of the cottage, Amber and Celeste worked in tandem converting the coven's stockpile of quicksilver daggers into witchblades. They made a baker's dozen each before hitting their deadline. Amber felt lightheaded from the strain of the work. She kicked herself for not taking some of her dad's stew when he offered.

"I'm going to go get us something to eat. You okay with a veggie sandwich?"

"Sounds divine." Celeste sat on the couch then kicked her feet up on the table.

"Be right back."

Amber slipped up the stairs to the living room where Jasmine was meeting with the coven's runners, the Sinclaire sisters. The three sisters were the best of the guilds. Each of the nobles belonged to a different guild and were loyal to the freedom movement. As one of the oldest families in Detroit, they were well respected. Their participation gave authenticity to the freedom movement. They were Jasmine's recruits. Amber only knew them because of their chain of bakeries, Sinclaire's Sweets.

"How's it going down there?" Jasmine asked.

"Done. Just grabbing something to eat."

"Good. We're going over the distribution plan."

Amber walked to the table to look at the street map of Witchtown. Jasmine had drawn two circles in red ink. The sisters were going to work out of their Witchtown bakeries, one on the westside and the other on the eastside. They'd gotten word out through the whisper network about the plan to break the cuffs. They'd set up a series of private invitation-only tasting events to host the breaking. *Medusa, protect the secrecy charm and keep the truth from unfriendly ears.*

"Looks good. Where's Zerrick?"

"Out back practicing his shifting. He's the cutest little grey wolf."

"Cute, huh? Jasmine and Zerrick sitting in a tre—"

The sisters giggled in harmony like a chorus.

"Shut up! Go bother Kane. We need to work." Jasmine shooed her away.

Amber mockingly held up her hands then walked into the kitchen.

Kane leaned on the counter, watching his tablet. Amber went to his side, mirroring his posture. The counter was cool to the touch, a welcome relief to the ache in her arms.

"The play is almost over. Are the witchblades done?"

"Yeah. I came to get something to eat."

"Handled." He nodded at two plates piled with mini quiches and hand pies. "I was going to bring it down, but I didn't want to interrupt. When I peeked in on you, you were in the zone."

"You did all this for us?"

"Yeah. I figured you needed something after all that work." Kane shrugged. "It wasn't that much work. The Sinclaires brought all the food. I just made a little plate."

"Thank you," she bumped him with her shoulder.

"Anything, always." He leaned over and kissed her cheek. "Helluva a day, huh?"

Heat rushed to the spot where his lips lingered a little too long for it to be innocent. Amber pushed the thought away. There wasn't any time for her childish crush. He was always worried about her. This didn't mean anything.

"Yeah. We've been so busy with the rescue missions and hunter attacks that I haven't had a chance to stop and think until now."

"What's on your mind?"

"We're missing something. My mom said the king and Nevin have been meeting secretly. And Rynn said Gavin was talking about clockwork guards."

"She mentioned Ediston. Maybe that's someone they are working with."

"Makes sense. But why a wind city? What does that even mean? Gavin's dad is water guildmaster."

"Maybe they're working with Jasmine's dad on something. Or plotting against him. Gavin did ask if Jasmine was single. Guess that's not an issue anymore."

"Guess not." Amber chuckled. "I can't believe they really thought I was just going to roll over and marry him."

"I'm glad you didn't." Kane put his hand on hers. He traced the outline of her marriage mark with his thumb. "Really glad. Amber, I lo—"

"Ahh. This is why I had to come get my own food," Celeste said.

Amber jumped. She turned toward Celeste's voice. She was standing in the door, arms crossed. A smirk played on her lips.

"Sorry! We were ju—"

Amber waved her hand at the tablet. *Shit. No more distractions.*

"Mmhmm." Celeste waved a dismissive hand at them. "I was young and in love once. I get it." She walked to the counter and grabbed two hand pies.

"We were watching the play." Kane stood up. "It's time to go."

"Good. Jasmine is gathering the witchblades for the sisters."

"You're clear on the plan?" Amber gobbled down a hand pie.

"Don't worry about me. I know what to do. This isn't my first coup. I won't make the same mistake twice."

Amber hoped she didn't. Letting King Wesley live after finding out what he was doing to the witchfolk had been a grave mistake for the kingdom. They had no interest in repeating the mistakes of the past. The king would fall. She hoped the queen didn't get in her way.

24

They walked through the portal into the king's study. Amber needed to see what the king was plotting. The royal procession had not arrived yet so there was time to do some quick snooping. Jasmine helped her search through the papers on his desk while Zerrick, Kane, and Celeste kept lookout at the door and windows.

"Tell me again what Rynn said. Exactly." Jasmine said.

"Gavin was talking to Jack about a city of wind, clockwork butlers, and Ediston."

"Edison? My dad had a newspaper that was talking about him. Apparently, he's some kind of American wizard."

"What? When did the Americans get magic?"

"I don't know. Jasmine shuffled through a pile of papers. "He seemed irritated by it. But he's always irritated."

Amber sifted through the drawers on the left side of the desk. There were only gadgets and trinkets, no paper. She closed the drawer and tapped Jasmine on the shoulder. They switched places. The right side of the desk was more of the same. Maybe this was a waste of time.

"Here! Look at this." Jasmine showed her a white folder with newspaper clippings and letters. "This is the same news article about Edison my dad had."

"Edison the Wizard. His Marvelous Inventions will be Exhibited in Chicago, the windy city." Amber read the headline aloud. "That answers that."

"Here's an invitation to something called the World Fair in Chicago." Jasmine flipped it over. "This is a personal invitation to Elios from the deputy governor of Illinois. They must be connected."

"What is a World Fair?" Amber asked.

"I don't know but it seems important to Elios. This whole folder is filled with papers talking about it."

"The procession is arriving," Zerrick said from the window.

"Bring those with us. We'll make the king tell us about them." Amber hurried to Kane's side. "We need to get to the drawing room now."

Kane nodded and jumped into action. In a flash, he wrote the portal charms on the door frame. Amber was the last one through the door. In front of her, Nazim's head bounced against Zerrick's back. The spare prince almost looked innocent while unconscious and being carried like a sack of potatoes. But he was a killer. She couldn't forget that. His time with the boneheads had been successful by their standards. Amber gladly would've left him in the stonegarden to rot next to Gavin if he wasn't a bargaining chip.

Her pulse quickened as they ran across the room to hide in the butler's pantry. The drawing room was gaudier than she remembered. The king had made some new additions. It was filled with oversized furniture upholstered in clashing plaid and striped patterns. On one wall, a brass grandfather clock stood between two waist-high dragon statues. The clock's gears groaned and glowed orange with each minute that passed.

After every foxhunt, the king enjoyed a drink with the guildmasters to discuss the mages' wins and losses. It was in those meetings that the fate of the guild was decided. Who would get special appointments or be dismissed outright. There was no room for weakness in the guild. Just after Amber's twelfth birthday, Amber and Kane had hidden in the butler's pantry to eavesdrop on guild gossip. They wanted insider info on the academy to know what school would be like. It was then that they learned the king was cruel. Their childish admiration of the guilds and academy were destroyed after only one snooping session. After her royal lessons started with the king, Amber realized the king was also a coward who feared witchfolk more than he loved taking their power.

Amber stepped into the butler's pantry. Another new addition stood in the corner: a clockwork butler. The machine appeared to be off. Its quartz eyes stared blankly, and its gears stood at a standstill. She'd never seen one of the machines powered down. It looked like an over-sized kid's toy.

They pantry was the size of the cottage's kitchen. Jasmine and Celeste stood at the back of the pantry. Jasmine and the queen weren't going to come out until the king was secured. Zerrick sat Nazim's body on the floor in the corner next to the butler. His head sagged against its copper knees. Amber took her position on the left side of the door opposite Kane. He tossed her a palm-sized seashell. A tiny bloodstone was nestled in the center of the spiral. She tucked the small spiral into her ear. They locked eyes and he mouthed, "Breathe." She nodded. They took a few synchronized breaths, silently. On the fourth exhale, he wrote the eavesdrop spell on the door. The ticking sounds of the clock shifted from muffled to crystal clear.

Within a minute, the main door opened accompanied by the sound of footsteps and a jumble of chatter. She closed her eyes, working to separate the voices. It was like picking out individual instruments in the orchestra. Nevin's husky laugh. Clayton's nasal droning. Elios' clipped baritone. Her mom's velvety voice. It was the only one that mattered. If they missed the signal, all their work would be wasted.

"So, we are in agreement? The Mori boy is dismissed from fire guild," Elios said.

"Yes. He is a coward and doesn't represent what the guild values," Clayton said.

"Running out of the labyrinth without putting up a fight. Maybe he needs some time in the mines to toughen him up," Nevin said.

"The boy did nothing wrong," Selene said.

"Good thing we don't need your vote."

"Seems to be a common occurrence lately."

"What does that mean?"

"It means I find it strange that the betrothal was announced the same day my daughter's guild license was denied because she's unmarried."

"You're paranoid."

"Sounds like good fortune to me," Elios said. "Speaking of my niece, where was she for the procession?"

"Today has been an emotionally taxing day, I'm sure she was just getting some air."

"Your royal *cage* stop working?" Nevin said. "Keeping her pinned up in that sky box seems cruel."

Shit. He definitely knew her secret. How many people had Gavin told?

"If anyone's child needs a cage, it's yours. The boy is a menace." Selene cleared her throat. "It's late. I will leave you all to it. I'm going *home*," Selene said.

Home. That was the signal.

Medusa, give me strength.

25

Amber nodded at Kane then pulled the eavesdropper out. Kane followed her through the door. They held their wands out as they walked toward the king. All noise in the room stopped. The king was seated in a plaid chair next to the grandfather clock. Nevin and Clayton sat on opposite ends of the couch across from him. Selene stood in the center of the room with her wand pointed at the king. Clayton walked to Selene's side with his wand raised. Nevin dropped his glass. Elios held up his hands in mock surrender. His eyes locked on Amber. She pointed a finger at him, the shadow of her griffin familiar stretching out and pinning him to the chair.

"There's no need for all this rage." Elios plastered a fake smile on his face. "We can talk through any grievance you all have."

"There is nothing you can say to fix what you've done," Selene said.

"Wands." Kane walked to each of them and disarmed them. Elios held his grip on the wand. "Don't be stupid your *majesty*." Kane snatched it away. He held out a hand until Elios put his charmtek ring and necklace in it.

"What do you want?" Elios' eyes darted between Amber and her mom.

"We'll start with your throne. If you answer our questions, I might let you live." Amber rolled Gavin's head to the king. "I brought you a *gift*. Consider it my bride-price."

Gavin's head wobbled then stopped at the king's feet. Gavin's stone eyes pointed at the ceiling. Elios recoiled from the stone.

"What is th—" Nevin cocked his head to the side. Recognition washed over him. He cried out in a rage. "Selene. Control your daughter. This is outrageous." His voice was strained.

"What's outrageous is that Gavin and Nazim attacked me tonight."

"That is an outlandish lie." The king hit the arm of his chair. "I will not sit here and listen to th—"

"Bring the prince," Amber shouted.

"I want this girl arrested!" Nevin yelled. "Now!"

"Be quiet!" Selene pressed her wand to his temple. "Or I will silence you. Your wife already has two funerals to plan, don't be stupid and make it three."

Zerrick carried in Nazim over his shoulder. The spare king was still under the sleeping spell. Jasmine and Celeste followed behind him. Clayton smiled and nodded at Jasmine.

"What have you done to him?" Elios demanded.

"Less than what he planned to do to me." Amber stepped closer to him. "He's fine for now. Now, it's up to you if he stays that way. One snap and he won't remember his own name."

"What do you want?" His jaw tightened.

"Your throne and the truth." Celeste stepped forward.

"Who are you?" Elios stared at the queen.

"You can call me grandmother." A wicked smile spread across her face.

"Enough games. Release my son and leave before I have you all stoned."

"That's not happening. The royal guards are ours," Kane said.

"Fire guild and air guild stand against you," Clayton said.

"You are sorely outnumbered. I would start answering their questions before things get really bad." Kane bent down and pressed a quicksilver dagger to Nazim's shoulder.

"Fine." Elios sighed. "What do you want to know?"

"Why did you kill my daughter?" Celeste asked.

"You mean to tell me this is truly the traitor witch queen?" Elios chuckled. His eyes darted between Celeste, Amber, and Selene. "Seriously?"

"I remade the witchblade." Amber pulled out the golden dagger. "Would you like to see how it works?"

Before he could answer, Kane cut Nazim. Elios tried to get up as the curse spread through the prince's body. Amber twisted her hand. Her spirit's hold on his shoulder tightened, holding him in the chair. Kane walked to Amber's side. His fingers brushed against her leg as he took the witchblade from her holster. *Was that an accident?* She shook of the tingling sensation where his hand had lingered. Two strides later, he dropped to a knee by Nazim. He plunged the witchblade into the prince's chest. The curse broke and the stone fell away. Nazim coughed and looked around with wide eyes. Kane hit him with the sleeping spell again.

"It can't be." Elios closed his eyes. "This isn't real."

"Oh, it is. Open your eyes coward," Celeste said. "I am very much real. Now, tell me. What. Did. You. Do. To. My. Child?"

"Nothing. It was an acci—"

"Stop lying. *Veritas dico.*" Jasmine cast the silvertongue spell. Her words snaked across the room and seeped into the king's ear. His eyes glossed over with an unnatural silver shimmer. The silvertongue spell was set. Jasmine nodded at Celeste. "You can ask now."

"How did you kill your mother?"

"A poisoned apple. It was...poetic."

"Why?" Celeste asked.

"The crone wouldn't give up the throne. Then when she told us she was going to give it to Selene, I had no choice. I wouldn't let her humiliate me like that. It was my right. Women have no place on the throne."

"You bastard! Mom protected you from dad and this is how you repaid her." Selene shook her head. "A dog would make a better king than you. At least they are loyal."

"Every time she stepped in to *protect* me, she made me look weak. That's why I killed him. He knew I wasn't weak in the end when I snapped his neck."

"Both of our parents. Both? All for that little crown?" She flicked her wand at him, sending the crown crashing into the wall. "I should've ended your miserable life when I took your ear."

"You don't have the guts to kill me."

"You're right. I don't but Amber does. And she has every right after what you did to her," Selene chuckled. "You know, I thought jail would be enough of a punishment for you. I was wrong." She turned to Amber, "Do whatever you want with him. I'm done. He can't be saved."

Amber's heart ached at the pain in her mom's voice. They knew the truth about her mom but finding out the king's death hadn't been an accident was too much to bear. She nodded at Jasmine.

"What is the World Fair? Who is Edison the wizard?" Jasmine asked.

"An American conman. He has the Americans convinced he's the best inventor in the world. That's what their little fair is for. It's a showcase of so-called inventions to celebrate the birth of their nation. Their little toys are nothing compared to what I've been doing here for years. Charmtek is more advanced than their wildest dreams. They'll see that when I'm done."

"What do mean? Done with what?" Amber asked. "Kingslaw prohibits contact with the Americans."

"Do not quote the book to me. I *am* Kingslaw! The time of isolation is over. The Americans are arrogant. It's time for them to be put in their place. When I kill that fool Edison the Americans will come begging for Charmtek. This will cha—"

The king's eyes cleared. Jasmine stumbled backwards into Zerrick who caught her with one arm. Elios looked around the room. A light shadow crossed his face. He spit on the floor. Kane pointed his wand at him. Celeste held up a shaking hand.

"Your questions are answered. Let Nazim go. I'll forgive all th—"

"I'm sorry. Maybe you aren't understanding what's happening here." Amber took a step closer. "Step down or get taken out. Your choice. We have the witchblade. You can't torture the witchfolk anymore. There's no reason for anyone to fear you."

"You're wrong." Elios smiled. "You will always have a reason to fear me." The king touched a button on his shirt. A halo of orange light glowed around him like fog.

Amber blinked. *What the hell?* When the light faded, his chair was empty. The king was gone. *Hell no.*

26

Four hours of searching confirmed her worst fear. The king wasn't in the palace. The plan failed. Amber paced the war room. *Should've known the coward would run. Shit.* Her familiar roared inside her head. The coven was gathered at the far end of the room around the meeting table. Her mom and Imani had been arguing for the better part of the last hour. She joined Kane at the window. The city stretched out before her in a mass of gleaming glass and marble. Warm rays of the rising sun streamed on her face.

"I thought I disarmed him." Kane's voice was distant. "I failed you. I'm sorry."

"You've never failed me, Kane." She reached out and held his hand. "Don't ever think that this was your fault. None of us knew he had portal gems. Not even me. Whatever the enchantment is that he uses on them, their aura is unreadable."

"Thank you." He interlaced his fingers with hers. "Where do you think he went?"

"I don't know but I'll never stop until I find him. He *will* pay for his crimes."

"I'll be at your side every step of the way." He squeezed her hand. "Always."

"This is my burden. You don—"

"I love you. Your burden is mine to bear." He turned to face her. "You don't have to love me back. That's not why I told you. I just needed to say it. I've been holding it in too long."

"I love you too. How long you been holding out on me?" She bumped him with her shoulder.

"Oh, not too long. Just since we were thirteen."

His timing was horrible, but she couldn't help but grin.

"The kiss?"

"The kiss." He nodded.

"Me too. I thought it meant nothing to you, so I stayed quiet."

"It was everything." He traced small circles on her hand.

"Well, that's good because we're stuck together now."

"Wouldn't have it any other way."

"Are you two done?" Imani called out, "we need to talk."

"That's our cue." He leaned over and kissed her cheek.

All eyes were on them as they crossed the room. Amber tucked her hands in her pockets, heat flushed her cheeks. They sat side-by-side at the round mahogany table between Jasmine and Celeste.

"Tonight was obviously not what any of us expected or wanted. Nothing will be accomplished by assigning blame. It's best to move forward. We have decisions to make." Selene cleared her throat. "We must decide what to do with the royal twins. Obviously, we can't put Nazim on the throne. He doesn't remember much but he still was a bonehead and that can't be forgiven. The question of Maximo is more complicated."

"He's always been a kind-hearted boy. But I fear that's not enough to trust him." Imani added. "Plus, he's still in the academy. Having an untrained mage on the throne is an issue."

"So, we pick a regent until he is ready," Amber said. "Mom, you can do it right?"

"No. The guild needs me now. We already have to replace Nevin and appoint someone to run the earth guild. We need a bit of consistency in the chaos. The choice is you or Celeste, dear. What do you want?"

Amber's head swirled. The throne wasn't her fate. *Just another cage. No thank you.*

"I want to hunt the bastard down. He can't get away with what he's done."

"I figured as much." Selene sighed.

"That's for the best. The people will be inspired by queen Celeste. She is the awakened queen," Imani said. "There is no better way to show our stance against the stonings."

"And if they don't believe it? If it's all dismissed as rumor or legend? Then what? We leave the throne open to rebellion or worse. The kingdom is bigger than the city. We don't know all the threats that are out there. We don't know what the king is plotting."

"The king is gone. If he returns, we will get him to renounce the throne and step aside, *officially*." Imani looked around the table. "He won't escape a second time."

So much for not blaming anyone. Amber dropped her gaze to the table. She took the blame for their failure. She should've followed her gut and not their plan. They wanted to do things the right way. Getting the king to agree to give up the throne was a mistake. She should've unleashed the flame on him and been done with the whole affair.

"We need to find him first, before he can craft his own narrative," Selene said.

"Let me track him. I have hunter's stones. There can only be so many places to hide in the city," Amber said.

"He isn't in the city. When I questioned the guards, one of them confessed to helping him. Elios left in an airship. Apparently, it was waiting for him at the outskirts of the city," Tarkan said. "He must've used the portal gem to access it."

"So, he knew about our plan?" Fear crept into her chest. "How?"

"No. He was planning a secret trip to Chicago. The airship was supposed to leave after the foxhunt," Tarkan answered.

"I'm guessing he was going to make the announcement at the closing ceremony tonight. That's why this is complicated" Selene said. "If you want to hunt him, you'll have to travel into the American wastelands."

America. The land of fairytales and nightmares. She'd never considered going there before. It was a violent place, filled with horrors worse than anything in the kingdom.

"I'll go anywhere to find him."

"And I'll go anywhere to protect you," Kane said. "We can do this."

"We're going too." Jasmine put a hand on top of Zerrick's. "I can learn everything we need to know about America and the fair on the journey."

"What of the witchfolk and earth guild?" Zerrick asked.

"We have word from the Sinclaires that they are making progress on breaking as many cuffs as possible. They have good numbers so far. As for the earth guild, it will be restarted. I will be its guildmaster," Imani said. "At least until I can train a witch to take over."

"Rynn. She would be perfect. People trust her," Amber said.

"That is a fine pick." Selene nodded.

"What about the boneheads, Captain Vaughn? Were you able to find Jack and Pippy?" Amber chewed her bottom lip.

"No. They could be with the king. They could be in hiding. Some of the boneheads went to ground when we started rounding them up. There's about a dozen we haven't been able to find. We have their names and addresses from the crown records. Guards are posted outside their homes but the odds of them coming back are small."

One more thing to worry about.

"That's all for now. We have a few hours until the opening ceremony of the foxhunt. Everyone get some rest until then." Selene dismissed them with a flourish of her hand.

Amber didn't need to be told twice; she was exhausted. Her royal suite was on the other side of the palace but at the front of her mind.

To save her from walking across the entire building, Kane used the side door to open a portal to her bedroom.

"Thanks for letting me stay." Zerrick turned in a circle taking in the whole of her suite. He counted aloud as he pointed at each of the doors that led from the hexagonal common area. "You have five rooms? This is a definite upgrade from the temple dorms."

"Sort of. One is Jasmine's. One is Kane's. The other two are the sparring room and the kitchen."

"I'm officially impressed."

"It's really the only perk of living here. You can take Kane's room. Feel free to get something from the kitchen. I need to go pass out."

"Will do. I'm kinda hungry. I forgot shifting took so much energy. It's been years since I've been able to."

"Make yourself at home. You can use the sparring room if you want to shift some more."

"Thanks."

"I'll show you." Jasmine grabbed him by the hand. "See you guys soon." She led him away while gushing about her secret stash of lemon cookies.

"Oh, she's about to be really disappointed." Kane smirked.

"How do you always find all the hidden snacks?"

"It's a gift. Let's go before sh—"

"Kane! I swear to goddess..." Jasmine's voice trailed off.

"Too late." He pulled her into the room just as Jasmine walked through the door.

Amber smiled. It was just like the old times, before the torture, before the academy, before everything. She kicked off her shoes and went to her closet to change into her nightgown. When she came out Kane was halfway asleep on the bed. She crawled next to him, laying her head on his chest. Kane wrapped his arms around her and pulled her closer. She leaned into his embrace as his heart beat against hers. Without warning, fat hot tears ran down her face. Her heart ached for all that was lost. The king fled to the forbidden wastelands. Jack and Pippy were on the run. She closed her eyes hoping sleep would quiet her racing thoughts. At least the witchfolk were free and Gavin couldn't threaten her anymore.

Thank you, Medusa.

THE END

About the Author

Renae L. Moore grew up in Detroit. When she isn't gardening, she is reimagining history, dreaming of mythical creatures, and examining her belief in happily ever afters through fiction.

About the Author

Renae L. Moore grew up in Detroit. When she isn't gardening, she is reimagining history, dreaming of mythical creatures, and examining her belief in happily ever afters through fiction.

Read more at www.renaelmoore.com.

www.ingramcontent.com/pod-product-compliance
Lightning Source LLC
Chambersburg PA
CBHW021101130626
46552CB00016B/2256